SPACE

Cosy Poems
Chosen by Gaby Morgan

Out There in the Wild
By James Carter, Dom Conlon and Nicola Davies
Illustrated by Diana Catchpole

Gods and Monsters: Mythological Poems
Chosen by Ana Sampson and
Illustrated by Chris Riddell

ROYAL
OBSERVATORY
GREENWICH

S P A C E

Royal Observatory Greenwich Poetry Book

Chosen by Gaby Morgan

MACMILLAN

Published 2025 by Macmillan Children's Books, an imprint of Pan Macmillan
The Smithson, 6 Briset Street, London EC1M 5NR
EU representative: Macmillan Publishers Ireland Ltd, 1st Floor,
The Liffey Trust Centre, 117–126 Sheriff Street Upper, Dublin 1 D01 YC43

In association with Royal Museums Greenwich, the group name for the
National Maritime Museum, the Royal Observatory, the Queen's House and *Cutty Sark*
Greenwich, London, SE10 9NF
rmg.co.uk

ISBN 978-1-0350-6826-5

1 3 5 7 9 8 6 4 2

A CIP catalogue record for this book is available from the British Library.

Printed and bound by CPI Group (UK) Ltd, Croydon CR0 4YY

Visit **www.panmacmillan.com** to read more about all our books and buy them.

For G, J, E, G and P – the whole universe xx

Contents

Sun/Stars 35

Universe

People   177

Time   219

Watercolour of the Royal Observatory, Greenwich from the south-east

Foreword

Let me tell you a story. It starts in 1675 with King Charles II and his order to build the Royal Observatory, Greenwich. It was to be the first purpose-built scientific organization ever to exist – exciting stuff indeed. A building like that doesn't run itself, so allow me to introduce the first 'astronomical observer' John Flamsteed. He took the reins in 1676 with a pretty big job ahead of him – to 'perfect the art of navigation' by first cataloguing the stars.

First things first, Flamsteed needed to create Greenwich Mean Time (GMT) to help him with his measurements. Little did he know quite how much of an impact he was going to have on all of our lives for the next two centuries. Unfortunately, Flamsteed's catalogue was impressive and groundbreaking but it was also very expensive, wildly technical and quite frankly enormous, so not very practical to take to sea.

Fast forward forty years, add the fifth Astronomer Royal, Nevil Maskelyne, and a sprinkle of help from assistants and 'human computers' and boom – major progress. You are probably wondering about 'human computers'. Well, they were people with absolutely wild maths skills who could perform calculations so easily and quickly they operated like human computers – the name now makes sense then, right? This group of people (along with some nifty new tools such as *The Nautical Almanac* (1767), a pocket watch and a sextant) worked out a way where you could know your position at sea . . . well, a little better at least.

That is a lot of scientific activity in a short space of time but, wait, there was more! All the while a group of clockmakers were beavering away trying to make a clock that could keep time at sea. This is not an easy task when a ship is throwing you around all over the place, it took some major thought and lots of people believed they had the answer. John Harrison eventually created H4 and proved that it could be done – hooray! The Admiralty then gave the Royal Observatory the challenge to test chronometers (sea clocks) against the clocks on land by observing the stars to check their accuracy. This combination of skills cemented the Observatory as a very useful and scientifically important place to have at your disposal. This is why the Observatory became the front-runner when deciding where to measure time from in the world, because we had GMT and the Greenwich Meridian.

It took a long time, the competition was tough and there were highs and lows along the way but the Royal

Observatory, Greenwich, has become a true historical and scientific icon through the amazing work its people have done.

Space is pretty bonkers when you think about it . . . Unimaginable vastness filled with wonder, possibilities for exploration and the mind-boggling unknown. As astronomers these are things that really get our thoughts racing and our hearts pumping. We use the evidence we collect as an international community to help us make sense of the universe and how it works. Together we have made incredible discoveries that have turned the scientific world on its head by asking big, challenging questions.

This has helped to build a picture of what we know is out there as well as new potential challenges. But it doesn't help us work out how we feel about it all. That is where getting creative can help. It is about letting your brain have some time to run free. It can even help to explain really difficult things, especially when we share our creations with others.

Elizabeth Avery

Deputy Head of Astronomy,
Royal Museums Greenwich

THE GREAT EQUATORIAL TELESCOPE IN THE DOME, GREENWICH OBSERVATORY.

The Great Equatorial Telescope which occupied the dome at the Royal Observatory, Greenwich from 1859 until 1893

Telescope

Aberration

The Hubble Space Telescope before repair.

The way they tell it
All the stars have wings
The sky so full of wings
There is no sky
And just for a moment
You forget
The error and the crimped
Paths of light
And you see it
The immense migration
And you hear the rush
The beating

Rebecca Elson

Extremely Large Telescope

We listen at the door of the room,
the Universe has just made its grand
entrance, the energetic reception
flattens the walls, creates new dimensions.

A jazz band is getting ready to play
the next number, wiping spit
from its mouthpiece; expectation
has its own gravitational pull.

So this is a night, the first one, already
cooling. But the crowd still expanding, pushing out.

Light plays the darling, rumouring
through the crowd. We watch it shrink
to hear-say; histories glint in glass eyes.

The lone note of a trumpet drifts
down between the years, its wave and
bounce barely stirring the bluesy smoke.

This far back everything shimmers.
We must get here earlier next time, we say,
as the Universe milks faint applause.

Vicki Husband

Star-Gazers

What crowd is this? what have we here! we must not
    pass it by;
A Telescope upon its frame, and pointed to the sky:
Long is it as a barber's pole, or mast of little boat,
Some little pleasure-skiff, that doth on Thames's
    waters float.

The Showman chooses well his place, 'tis Leicester's
    busy Square;
And is as happy in his night, for the heavens are blue
    and fair;
Calm, though impatient, is the crowd; each stands
    ready with the fee,
And envies him that's looking; – what an insight must
    it be!

Yet, Showman, where can lie the cause? Shall thy
    Implement have blame,
A boaster that, when he is tried, fails, and is put to
    shame?
Or is it good as others are, and be their eyes in fault?
Their eyes, or minds? or, finally, is yon resplendent
    vault?

An astronomer and his assistant operating the Great Equatorial Telescope, which is still in use today

Is nothing of that radiant pomp so good as we have here?
Or gives a thing but small delight that never can be dear?
The silver moon with all her vales, and hills of
     mightiest fame,
Doth she betray us when they're seen? or are they but
     a name?

Or is it rather that Conceit rapacious is and strong,
And bounty never yields so much but it seems to do
     her wrong?
Or is it that, when human Souls a journey long have had
And are returned into themselves, they cannot but be
     sad?

Or must we be constrained to think that these
     Spectators rude,
Poor in estate, of manners base, men of the multitude,
Have souls which never yet have risen, and therefore
     prostrate lie?
No, no, this cannot be; – men thirst for power and
     majesty!

Does, then, a deep and earnest thought the blissful
  mind employ
Of him who gazes, or has gazed? a grave and steady joy,
That doth reject all show of pride, admits no outward
  sign,
Because not of this noisy world, but silent and divine!

Whatever be the cause, 'tis sure that they who pry
  and pore
Seem to meet with little gain, seem less happy than
  before:
One after One they take their turn, nor have I one espied
That doth not slackly go away, as if dissatisfied.

William Wordsworth

The Leviathan's Eye

It was the coopers made the body of it,
A barrel, long as whale.
Then the blacksmiths for the smelting;
Took some burning I can tell you –
The peat for miles around was dug down to the rock –
Four tonnes of silver!
No, eight because there was two mirrors,
They misted like buttermilk in this air
So twas always one being polished whilst the other
    worked.
Then the carpenters for the ladders and the staging
And train men for the rails to carry the mirror from
    its buffing.

Imagine it, that silver eye
Seated in its giant tube looking up into the sky!
Not many got to see what it saw.
But me, I was just a boy back then
and the Earl, he was fond of children,
Having lost so many of his own.
He let me fetch and carry for him
in the long nights of *observation*.
And once gave me look:
Oh the blackness!
Oh the brightness!

And this, swirl of light!
I felt I'd fallen through the creature's eye
Into eternity.

Nicola Davies

On the eve of the Irish Famine, William Parsons, Fourth Earl of Rosse, of County Offaly, built the first astronomical telescope to see an object outside our own galaxy. He used the skills and resources available to him locally to make an instrument with groundbreaking abilities of observation. The drawings he made of galaxy M51, the Whirlpool Galaxy, were not superseded until the 1950s. His giant telescope was known by local people as the Leviathan of Parsonstown.

Telescope

We peer back in time with hexagonal mirrors,
thinly cloaked in gold.
Gazing at stars that died long ago,
we guess what our future might hold.

We follow the light to the edge of existence,
the gap between galaxies growing.
I wonder, once *our* star goes dark –
will someone peer back at the glowing?

Lisa Varchol Perron

The Octagon Room, the Royal Observatory, Greenwich, 1712

Telescope

O
telescOpe
telescOpe
shOw me
hOw
the mOon
glOws
shOw me
whO
the wOrld
knOws
shOw me
the prOgress
Of
thOse
skybOund
bOdies
frOm the
PlOugh to
cOld
Old
PlutO
shOw me
telescOpe
shOw me
the wOnders
that revOlve
beyOnd
yOur
cOol
pOlished
O

Kate Wakeling

Vera's Questions

Through the telescope
in her bedroom window,
ten-year-old Vera
looks at the night sky.

She sees the bright stars,
but also, the darkness.

What does it do?
The darkness.
Why is it there?
The darkness.
How does it work?
Vera's questions
multiply.

When she gets older,
the men want to take
away Vera's telescope.
Women can't be
astronomers, they say.

Vera keeps
looking at the night sky.
She keeps
wondering what and why.

Using the world's largest
telescope, she begins
to find answers.

The darkness is matter.
The darkness is energy.
Pulling stars into galaxies.
Building the universe.

But how, and why?

Amidst the bright stars
and the darkness,
Vera's questions
multiply.

Ann Malaspina

Father Christmas Sent Me to the Moon

I don't know how he put it there:
our gas fire blocked the chimney
and the green rug where I played
had never magically flown for me.

But there it was – a telescope,
unwrapped but still a mystery,
centred like a compass needle
pointing the way to my heart.

I lifted it to the window, lowered its legs
like a newborn lamb's and opened
its eye to a world still waiting
to be cratered by snowballs.

I took my first footsteps before I could breathe,
when I looked at the Moon and learned to believe.

Dom Conlon

In My Sights

My telescope
A cardboard toilet roll
Didn't do the job
Far away was still far away

Grandad's though
In his upstairs window
Pointed to the skies
And brought outer space
Very much into my space

And then, to London
The Royal Observatory
And the Great Equatorial Telescope
Over eight metres long
And a lens nearly a metre wide
And . . .

Wow!
Just eye-poppingly wow!
The distant mysterious
Became so clear
Stars so close
Almost touchable
Planets you feel you could hold

Thanks to this telescope
Two worlds collide

Paul Cookson

Kepler

Kepler
Your mission was to search for planets
Orbiting stars outside our solar system
You found them

Kepler
Planet hunter
Investigator Extraordinaire
Good work

Kepler
Your sense of duty was admirable
You never once wavered from your task
We salute you

Kepler Telescope
We thank you for the legacy you have left us
Rest now, Kepler
Goodnight

Debra Bertulis

The Kepler Space Telescope (named after German astronomer Johannes Kepler) was launched by NASA in 2009 to find exoplanets, planets that exist outside our solar system. Kepler's epic mission revolutionized scientists' understanding of our universe. Kepler was quite the hero!

ROYAL OBSERVATORY GREENWICH.

To the Rev.d D.r Maskelyne, This Plate is Inscribed, by his obliged Servant, J. Baker.

A view of the Royal Observatory, Greenwich from the north

Greenwich

The Myths of Space

Imagine yourself back to centuries ago,
when Greenwich had no proper name;
when it lay quiet beside a river, in darkness,
lit only by a blazing moon, full-faced and round.
Imagine ships, long-oared, creeping
upriver on a rising neap tide, laden with
Roman soldiers, (even an armoured elephant),
intent on conquest. How did they find the long way
from Tiber's banks, from Ostia to Father Thames?
Their stars were the same as ours, but
they had no fancy telescopes to spy them with.
They mapped their night skies with celestial Beings,
inhabitants from far off myth –
old Jupiter, bright Venus of the dawn and dusk,
Orion belted with stars, hunter and hunted,
the seven Dancing Pleiades – drawing patterns
to navigate by, the static North Star guiding
their way through seas both rough and calm,
to this sea-girt island of ours, without knowledge
of latitude or longitude, caught by currents
of war, never knowing that men would later on
in this same spot divide the sky with algebra
and lenses made of convex glass.

Lucy Coats

JOHANNES FLAMSTEEDIUS *Derbiensis*
Astronomiæ Professor Regius. Anno Ætatis 74 Obijt
Decem. 31 1719

Engraving of John Flamsteed, appointed first Astronomer
Royal with the founding of the Royal Observatory in 1675

King Charles Discusses His Royal Observatory

We built it in my Royal Park
to see stars shining in the dark.

It sits on top of Greenwich Hill
a fine design from Wren's neat quill.

The grandest room is tall and straight
six sides he thought. I made that eight.

I filled it with amazing clocks
chiming, rhyming loud tick-tocks.

We need, I said, a telescope
and a clever fellow, not some dope.

Let us find a mathematician
a star-gazing genius, with erudition.

You think John Flamsteed? Just the chap
to make some charts, perhaps a map?

He's clever but keeps droning on
about some mistakes. I said, Look John

Don't bother me, I need a rest
if the room's all wrong, just do your best.*

Be quiet now, please don't yell
if you have to Flamsteed, dig a well.

Going down a hundred feet?
A telescope longer than a street!

Lie on your back if you must
you'll find the damp will make things rust.

If that's no good John, don't despair
go round the back, the answer's there.

See what I mean, a small brick shed?
Start counting stars from there instead.

David Harmer

Unfortunately, the Octagon Room didn't line up with the stars properly. The Astronomer Royal, John Flamsteed, had a well dug and his telescope installed vertically. He sat underneath it a few times but the instrument was ruined by damp, so he made his observations from a small shed instead.

Engraving of the Royal Observatory in Greenwich, about 1750

On a Hill in Greenwich

On a hill in Greenwich
children can be clearly seen
without the need of a telescope.

They are on a school trip
dreaming of space and seas
and time's arrow.

It is written in the stars
that one of them
will be an amateur astronomer

one of them
will be a professional astronomer
and one will be a gardener.

Let's hope all of them
have the chance
to reach for the stars.

Rob Walton

The Old Royal Observatory, Greenwich

You need time to see
All there is to see
At the Old Royal Observatory

In the octagonal room
The long pendulum of time
Swings slowly

And on a cool New Year's Eve
You find yourself
Standing on the frost-flecked slopes

Of Observatory Hill
Watching for the second
Which every year escapes

But the new-fangled atomic clock
Loses only one second
Every billion years

And you find yourself wondering
How can we live
With such a gaping margin of error?

Roger Stevens

Photograph of the Altazimuth Building, the Royal
Observatory, Greenwich

Diary Entry, Greenwich – 10 August 1675

Tonight, my friends,
I sit beneath the stars.
And tomorrow,
and for as many as I can fathom.

I plot and chart this wondrous abyss
that leaves oceans as puddles.

Tonight, I observe
this compelling moon:
it takes residence
in my retinas.

Tonight, I begin the translation
of that which transcends existence.

I shall be sure to make myself comfy
on a voyage
that appears to be
infinite.

Matt Abbott

In the Chapel-Like Perfection of the Royal Observatory

perched high overlooking Blackheath,
designed by polymath Sir Christopher Wren,
the wedding takes place of Astronomy and Philosophy
with Artistry and Horology for bridesmaids,
page boys are Mathematics and Cartography.
Stars twinkle in their millions
while those plump-cheeked zephyrs on the charts
writhing krakens and leviathans
dance to the music of the spheres.

That was three hundred years ago, and yet,
here in the dark sky zone of East Cornwall
with an upward gaze and the naked eye
I follow the track of a distant satellite,
knowing that electro-magnets and computers rule,
but somehow the triumphant survivors of that
great Renaissance flowering, Awe and Wonder
still draw me in under the jewelled
clear night canopy.

Jane Newberry

Photograph of dust clouds in the constellation Cepheus by
Oleg Bryzgalov, 2011

Sun/Stars

A Small Star

I live on a small star
Which it is my job to look after;
It whirls through space
Wrapped in a cloak of water.

It is a wonderful star:
Wherever you look there is life,
Though it's held at either end
In a white fist of ice.

There are creatures that move
Through air, sea and earth,
And growing things everywhere
Make beauty from dirt.

Everything is alive!
Even the very stones:
Amazing crystals grow
Deep under the ground.

And all the things belong,
Each one to the other.
I live on a precious star
Which it is my job to look after.

Gerard Benson

He Wishes for the Cloths of Heaven

Had I the heavens' embroider'd cloths,
Enwrought with golden and silver light,
The blue and the dim and the dark cloths
Of night and light and the half light;
I would spread the cloths under your feet:
But I, being poor, have only my dreams;
I have spread my dreams under your feet;
Tread softly because you tread on my dreams.

W. B. Yeats

Love

We two that planets erst had been
Are now a double star,
And in the heavens may be seen,
Where that we fixèd are.

Yet, whirled with subtle power along,
Into new space we enter,
And evermore with spheral song
Revolve about one centre.

Henry David Thoreau

The Spacious Firmament on High

The spacious firmament on high,
With all the blue ethereal sky,
And spangled heavens, a shining frame
Their great Original proclaim.
Th'unwearied sun, from day to day,
Does his creator's powers display,
And publishes to every land
The work of an almighty hand.

Soon as the evening shades prevail
The moon takes up the wondrous tale,
And nightly to the listening earth
Repeats the story of her birth;
While all the stars that round her burn
And all the planets in their turn,
Confirm the tidings as they roll,
And spread the truth from pole to pole.

Joseph Addison

Stargazing

Leave your front door
leave your streetlights
leave your red brakes   tight white beams

Leave your city
leave your townlet
leave your village   take your dreams

Cross an ocean
if you need to
cross a dust plain   railway track

Climb a shallow
scoop of mountain
lie down full length   on your back

under fruit trees
under black skies
insect roar   resounding lands

you have found
the place you looked for
where the universe   cupped hands

spills the Milky Way above you
fills your eyes
your heart

                    expands

your brain

                    elides

your fear

and fixes you
a diamond pinpoint

                  Star

in Constellation
Here

Imogen Russell Williams

To the Evening Star

Thou fair-hair'd Angel of the Evening,
Now, whilst the sun rests on the mountains, light
Thy bright torch of love: thy radiant crown
Put on, and smile upon our evening bed!
Smile on our loves: and whilst thou drawest the
Blue curtains of the sky, scatter thy silver dew
On every flower that shuts its sweet eyes
In timely sleep. Let thy west wind sleep on
The lake: speak silence with thy glimmering eyes,
And wash the dusk with silver. Soon, full soon,
Dost thou withdraw; then the wolf rages wide,
And then the lion glares through the dun forest.
The fleeces of our flocks are covered with
Thy sacred dew: protect them with thine influence!

William Blake

Stars

Stars
are to reach for,
beautiful freckles of hope,
speckles on velvet,
to steer ships,
to comfort those trapped
in the darkness of their making,
to lead the wayward when the compass falters,
to remind us that the day is almost breaking,
dawn is just out –
taking time to warm
the other side of the world.
Stars are for wishes.

Stars are
tiny lights of hope,
fireflies in the night,
golden specks to gaze at,
tin tacks on a dark cloth, studs glittering,
sequins on a first party dress.

Stars are
our brightest and best,
shards of hope to keep us going, marking the place,
making the seasons,
giving us reasons
because, somewhere out there,
there are other stargazers
gazing back.

Pie Corbett

Animals Name the Constellations

What's in the stars up above?
asked Sparrow of her brother.
It's the Egg in the Black Nest,
the Wing and Feather.
Have they been there long?
Forever my love, forever.

What's in the stars up above?
asked Tadpole of his father.
It's Silver Spawn in the Black Pond,
the Lily, Carp and Beaver.
Have they been there long?
Forever my love, forever.

What's in the stars up above?
asked Elephant of his sister.
It's the Herd in the Black Plain,
the Tusk, Trunk and River.
Have they been there long?
Forever my love, forever.

What's in the stars up above?
asked the Whale of her mother.
It's the Great Net in the Black Sea,
the lights of the Hunting Ship.
Have they been there long?
Forever my love, dive deep.

Mandy Coe

A Starry Night

A cloud fell down from the heavens,
    And broke on the mountain's brow;
It scattered the dusky fragments
    All over the vale below.

The moon and the stars were anxious
    To know what its fate might be;
So they rushed to the azure op'ning,
    And all peered down to see.

Paul Laurence Dunbar

Out in the Dark

Out in the dark over the snow
The fallow fawns invisible go
With the fallow doe;
And the winds blow
Fast as the stars are slow.

Stealthily the dark haunts round
And, when a lamp goes, without sound
At a swifter bound
Than the swiftest hound,
Arrives, and all else is drowned;

And I and star and wind and deer
Are in the dark together, – near,
Yet far, – and fear
Drums on my ear
In that sage company drear.

How weak and little is the light,
All the universe of sight,
Love and delight,
Before the might,
If you love it not, of night.

Edward Thomas

Always

The stars are always there
Even when they're not bright-glistening
So if things feel dark or lonely
Trust that someone's always listening

The earth is always turning
And the planets always spinning
And with each sun that soars or sinks
New chances are beginning

So make that wish upon a star
Even when they're not in view
The sun's bright light might hide them
But the stars are *always* there for you

Rhiannon Oliver

The Starlight Night

Look at the stars! look, look up at the skies!
   O look at all the fire-folk sitting in the air!
   The bright boroughs, the circle-citadels there!
Down in dim woods the diamond delves! the elves' – eyes!
The grey lawns cold where gold, where quickgold lies!
   Wind-beat whitebeam! air abeles set on a flare!
   Flake-doves sent floating forth at a farmyard scare! –
Ah well! it is all a purchase, all is a prize.

Buy then! bid then! – What? – Prayer, patience, alms, vows.
Look, look: a May-mess, like on orchard boughs!
   Look! March-bloom, like on mealed-with-yellow sallows!
These are indeed the barn; withindoors house
The shocks. This piece-bright paling shuts the spouse
   Christ home, Christ and his mother and all his hallows.

Gerard Manley Hopkins

Gazing Puzzle

When you gaze at me

You are watching history

I light your path

But I am a mystery

I am an actor

I am the sun

If you guess me

Then *you* are one

a star

Roger Stevens

Bright Star

Bright star, would I were steadfast as thou art –
Not in lone splendour hung aloft the night
And watching, with eternal lids apart,
Like nature's patient, sleepless eremite,
The moving waters at their priestlike task
Of pure ablution round earth's human shores,
Or gazing on the new soft-fallen mask
Of snow upon the mountains and the moors –
No – yet still steadfast, still unchangeable,
Pillow'd upon my fair love's ripening breast,
To feel for ever its soft fall and swell,
Awake for ever in a sweet unrest,
Still, still to hear her tender-taken breath,
And so live ever – or else swoon to death.

John Keats

At Dieppe

After Sunset

The sea lies quieted beneath
The after-sunset flush
That leaves upon the heaped grey clouds
The grape's faint purple blush.

Pale, from a little space in heaven
Of delicate ivory,
The sickle-moon and one gold star
Look down upon the sea.

Arthur Symons

The Light of Stars

The night is come, but not too soon;
And sinking silently,
All silently, the little moon
Drops down behind the sky.

There is no light in earth or heaven
But the cold light of stars;
And the first watch of night is given
To the red planet Mars.

Is it the tender star of love?
The star of love and dreams?
O no! from that blue tent above,
A hero's armor gleams . . .

Henry Wadsworth Longfellow

93 Per Cent Stardust

(After Carl Sagan, who gave me hope as a child)

We have calcium in our bones,
iron in our veins,
carbon in our souls
and nitrogen in our brains.

93 per cent stardust,
with souls made of flames,
we are all just stars
that have people names.

Nikita Gill

Photograph of the Geminid meteor shower by Yu Lun, 2015

Komorebi

What throws a spotlight out to sea, a shaft brighter
    than an angel's gaze?
What calls the shoot from the split seed sleeping in
    the dark earth?
What draws the speckle of a robin's egg in freckles on
    a baby's nose?
What stripes the sky and speaks the patterns to an
    insect's brain?
What warms the adder basking on her stone?
What greens the leaf and casts the shadow of the tree?
What shines on every lifted face the hope of a new day?
It is the light from our home star, and when she rests
A million suns sparkle in the space she left.

Nicola Davies

Komorebi *is a Japanese word meaning sunlight coming through leaves.*

Your Host Today . . .

Ladies and gentlemen
Torches away please,
It's nearly time to welcome our
Awesome host for the day . . .

A reminder to please show respect
At all times, and do keep your distance
For fear of burns to the skin, retina,
Indeed, everything you own.

Here she comes,
Our long-serving star,
Creeping into sight,
Currently around 4.6 billion years young
And still luminous, dazzling, invigorating,
Still holding everything together for us all.

She's vital, she's energizing,
She's frankly enormous –
Ladies and Gentlemen,
Please give a great big earth '*Good Morning*' to
The most famous star by far,
The *only* star in our solar system,
Stand by and let her make your day,
Your host . . .

The sun!

Rhiannon Oliver

The Sun is known as Earth's host star because its light and energy make life on Earth possible.

The Last Light of the Sun

The Last Light of the Sun
If the star that lights our world should someday
suddenly
and with no warning
blink out of existence
we would be unaware until
eight minutes
and twenty seconds more
had passed.
Then the final shining of the Sun would fall upon the
    Earth
and leave us here in darkness.
But that last light would live on
travelling across the vast black emptiness
touching Mars minutes later
Jupiter within the hour.
A few hours more to leave the solar system
four years or so to where our nearest astral neighbour
    blazes
and on, and on
the last moments of one star's history.
One day, perhaps
a younger race than ours
might give a new name to this yellow sun
place it in a constellation

observe it
theorize and learn about it
set it in mythology, in history, astronomy
study it across millennia
and never guess
that long, long, long before they ever saw it
it had ceased to be.

John Dougherty

The Star

Twinkle, twinkle, little star,
How I wonder what you are!
Up above the world so high,
Like a diamond in the sky.

When the blazing sun is gone,
When he nothing shines upon,
Then you show your little light,
Twinkle, twinkle, all the night.

Then the trav'ller in the dark,
Thanks you for your tiny spark,
He could not see which way to go,
If you did not twinkle so.

In the dark blue sky you keep,
And often thro' my curtains peep,
For you never shut your eye,
Till the sun is in the sky.

'Tis your bright and tiny spark,
Lights the trav'ller in the dark:
Tho' I know not what you are,
Twinkle, twinkle, little star.

Ann Taylor & Jane Taylor

Star!

Twinkle, twinkle little star
Scientists tell us what you are.
Hydrogen . . . and helium?
Oxygen and nitrogen . . .
Twinkle, twinkle little star
Is that really what you are?

Twinkle, twinkle, little spark
Bravely twinkling in the dark.
We come out to gaze at you,
when we worry what to do.
We find up there a ray of light.
A hope, a comfort in the night.
Twinkle, twinkle, little star!
Is hope and comfort what you are?

Twinkle, twinkle, I have a clue . . .
They say we're made of stardust too!
Made to shine, made to gleam,
to imagine and to dream.
Twinkle, twinkle, little star
– a friend to us is what you are.

Twinkle, twinkle, little child,
in the garden running wild.
Full of laughter, free and light.
I hope your future will be bright.
Twinkle Twinkle you'll go far
Shine on bravely – you're the star.

Michaela Morgan

Before I Close My Curtains

Every single night
before I close my curtains
after I've turned off
my bedside light
I kneel upon my bed
rest my elbows on the windowsill
and cradle in my palms
my sleepy, dreamy head

I always look up to see
if you are looking down at me
from your far-off galaxy
to see me looking up at you
from my tiny planet
from her fragile crust
of basalt and granite

Then
as your starry wink
4,000 light years away
twinkles in my glassy blink
I feel my inner space
and your outer space
sync

There's harmony
in you and me
star and boy
boy and star
wandering through the universe
pondering as we both traverse
why or what we are

Mark Bird

What the Sun Said

The sun said:

This is my bonfire eye

in a carbon-dark sky I flare and flame,

do not glare at me, do not gaze.

I am the furious inferno of the skies,

do not stare at me, not at my blaze.

My rays spray in all directions,

my heat touches bird and fish.

I construct life; I compose star, planet, universe!

My warmth is a simple, faltering wish.

John Rice

What the Moon Said

The moon said:

This is my silver mask.

I know I look frail, fragile even:

a touch tantalizing – huh, a fine disguise!

Think of me not as flimsy, nor feeble,

for I can blind your petty planet's eyes!

I'll heave and haul your oceans as a child

would drag a blanket across the floor.

Who has a stranglehold on planet Earth?

The sun? No, my moon-clasp for sure!

John Rice

What the Star Said

The star said:

This is my silvery brooch

clasped to a cloak as black as middlenight.

My light is never-ending like Time's own relation.

I move in the obscurity of a revolving emptiness,

burning dust, eating the crust of creation.

I am naught but a lit match on a dark island

almost seen by those so far from reach.

Me and my crowds of stars jittering!

We may appear in the shade of pear or peach,

but whatever colour we choose, you will see silver!

John Rice

Astronomical glass plate slide of open star cluster Pleiades

The Pleiades

Orion the Hunter heard music one night,
whilst out stalking deer in the fading light,
caught laughter and singing adrift on the breeze,
crept softly closer and peered through the trees.
Maia, Electra, Calaeno, Merope,
Alayone, Taygate and fair Asterope,
the daughters of Atlas, all twirling and swaying,
and Artemis, lovingly watching them playing.

They were dazzling and radiant,
        by moonlight they danced.
They sparkled with beauty.
        He was charmed and entranced.

A stick snapped. The dancers were startled, and fled.
Orion chased after. The girls kept ahead,
and Artemis raged and soon took affront,
as for seven long years he disturbed every hunt.
She pleaded with Zeus to do what he could,
to stop them being chased through wood after wood.
But the next night Orion again found the glade
where the sisters were laughing, unaware, unafraid.

They were dazzling and radiant,
        by moonlight they danced.
They sparkled with beauty.
        He was charmed and entranced.

Orion, the hunter, stepped into the light.
The sisters, the hunted, promptly took flight.
As they raced through the trees, their feet left the
    ground.
They'd been turned into pigeons! Orion looked round.
His quarry had vanished, flying fast, flying far,
as far as the heavens, where they all turned to stars.
And there they are still. Each autumn they rise,
the Pleiades. Seven sisters, kept safe in the skies.

Still dazzling and radiant,
        by moonlight still dancing.
Still sparkling with beauty.
        Still charming. Entrancing.

                            Jacqueline Shirtliff

Astronomical glass plate slide of the Moon, 1903

Moon

You

You intergalactic car crash,
You shrapnel of a bygone age,
You mother,
You watcher,
You God.

You who watched the Earth burn,
You who saw it reborn,
Who saw life spread.
You who called to dreamers,
To scientists,
To lovers,
To priests,
To kings.
You who called to us,

Every one of us,
From before time existed.

You who is constant,
Yet constantly changing.

You who calls to the seas
To set their rhythm,

Who tells these watery lungs
To breathe.

You who infiltrated dreams,
In every age of man,
Who asked artists
To do more,
To be more,
To be immortal,
Like you.

Jay Hulme

The Moon

The moon
has mountains and
craters where meteors collide;
no air or soundwaves, no heartbeats
no tide. Rock, ancient lava, stardust and
glass, no snow or colours, no clouds, soil
or grass. Her beauty's reflection, a grey rock
in space, she borrows the soft light that
shines from her face. Black sky and stars'
paths and sun are her view, and a slow
planet, turning, in white veils and blue.
And it seems mysterious, her
manner of birth – that she is the
daughter and part of
the earth.

Liz Brownlee

What If There Were No Moon?

There would be no months
A still sea
No spring tides
No bright nights
Occultations of the stars
No face
No moon songs
Terror of eclipse
No place to stand
And watch the Earth rise.

Rebecca Elson

Moons

Some people think of moons as children,
Eagerly racing but never straying
Far from their parent's side.

But really they are the mums,
They are the dads and their
Lives shrink whilst yours swells.

They watch volcanoes erupt,
Storms rage, ice creep and
Sunlight shine across your surface.

Mostly they stay quiet and close,
Guiding your tides and doing their best
To catch any meteors which might hurt you.

Then, at night, as half your face
Lies against its pillow, they tuck you in
And glow with pride.

Dom Conlon

The Mother Moon

The moon upon the wide sea
Placidly looks down,
Smiling with her mild face,
Though the ocean frown.
Clouds may dim her brightness,
But soon they pass away,
And she shines out, unaltered,
O'er the little waves at play.
So 'mid the storm or sunshine,
Wherever she may go,
Led on by her hidden power
The wild sea must plow.

As the tranquil evening moon
Looks on that restless sea,
So a mother's gentle face,
Little child, is watching thee.
Then banish every tempest,
Chase all your clouds away,
That smoothly and brightly
Your quiet heart may play.
Let cheerful looks and actions
Like shining ripples flow,
Following the mother's voice,
Singing as they go.

Louisa May Alcott

Moon Dance

One bright
silver apple hangs in the sky
and I am caught in a glow casting the
shadows like magic, turning the darkness
into a glittered light that lifts our cold souls
We are bathed in this lunar spell together
your hand in mine in the crisp night air
as moths we spiral, whirl and dance
lost in the moment and the
moonlight

Dawn McLachlan

Evening Shifts

As cloak-black clouds
of evening drift
across his torch-white eye,

the moon begins
his evening shift —
nightwatchman of the sky.

Graham Denton

The Moon

The Stars about the lovely moon
Fade back and vanish very soon,
When, round and full, her silver face
Swims into sight, and lights all space.

Sappho
Translated by Edwin Arnold

Moon-Mad

Look at the moon!
A crescent sky-ship sailing
out of a cloudy cocoon

Look at the moon!
A cauldron of amber
spelling, rain-come-soon

Look at the moon!
A Mexican gold plate
over Montezuma's tomb

Look at the moon!
A full-blown O
(I was trying to avoid the word balloon)

Just open the window of your room
and look at the wolf-raising
sea-swelling shape-shifting
myth-making
Earth-watching moon
holding us
in the bloom of a moon-lock

Grace Nichols

Sonnet to the Moon

The glitt'ring colours of the day are fled;
Come, melancholy orb! that dwell'st with night,
Come! and o'er earth thy wand'ring lustre shed,
Thy deepest shadow, and thy softest light;
To me congenial is the gloomy grove,
When with faint light the sloping uplands shine;
That gloom, those pensive rays alike I love,
Whose sadness seems in sympathy with mine!
But most for this, pale orb! thy beams are dear,
For this, benignant orb! I hail thee most:
That while I pour the unavailing tear,
And mourn that hope to me in youth is lost,
Thy light can visionary thoughts impart,
And lead the Muse to soothe a suff'ring heart.

Helen Maria Williams

Lady Moon

(How to tell her age)

O Lady Moon, your horns point towards the east –
    Shine, be increased;
O Lady Moon, your horns point towards the west –
    Wane, be at rest.

Christina Rossetti

One of a set of twelve astronomical prints first issued in 1846. This one shows the telescopic appearance of the Moon.

Native American Moons

Begin with the Wolf, howling
hunger in the night
when the Moon is full
and the Moon is fat
and the Moon holds all the light.   *January passes by.*

Shift to the Snow, casting
angels to the ground,
but the Wolf still hungers
and the Moon still hides
where all the food is found.   *February passes by.*

Watch for the Worm, pushing
through the Earth's veins
bringing growth
out of the dark
before the full Moon wanes.   *March passes by.*

Prepare for the Pink, calling
out an early Spring
for the Wolf must hunt
and the Wolf must eat
beneath the Moon's white wing.   *April passes by.*

Bend for the Flower, rising
up at the sight of the Sun,
at the heat of the land
and the cool of the Moon
as the Wolf finds strength to run.   *May passes by.*

Pluck the Strawberry, giving
its flesh for all to eat
now the world is awake
and the Moon is strong
and the year is half complete.   *June passes by.*

Run with the Buck, offering
new antlers to the sky
as the Wolf gives chase
and sun sets late
and the Moon remains close by.   *July passes by.*

Swim with the Sturgeon, teeming
in the water's wake,
wallow in abundance
rejoice in the day,
bathe in the Moon's red lake.   *August passes by.*

Bring in the Harvest, feeding
the farmer from Autumn's table,
gather the firewood
horde the light
share a moon-old fable.   *September passes by.*

Become the Hunter, preying
upon the fattened fox
as winter nears
and the Moon appears
inside night's darkest box.   *October passes by.*

Build with the Beaver, damming
the river against the rain,
fish can be caught
in moonlit currents
whilst the Wolf goes hungry again.   *November passes by.*

Carnival the Cold, freezing
the year long enough for us
to skate back
and catch
our moon memories in its flow.   *December passes by*
                                         as Wolf waits for
                                         the new year.

Dom Conlon

To the Autumnal Moon

Mild Splendour of the various-vested Night!
Mother of wildly-working visions! hail!
I watch thy gliding, while with watery light
Thy weak eye glimmers through a fleecy veil;
And when thou lovest thy pale orb to shroud
Behind the gather'd blackness lost on high;
And when thou dartest from the wind-rent cloud
Thy placid lightning o'er the awaken'd sky.

Ah such is Hope! as changeful and as fair!
Now dimly peering on the wistful sight;
Now hid behind the dragon-wing'd Despair:
But soon emerging in her radiant might
She o'er the sorrow-clouded breast of Care
Sails, like a meteor kindling in its flight.

Samuel Taylor Coleridge

Southern Night

Come up, thou red thing.
Come up, and be called a moon.

The mosquitoes are biting to-night
Like memories.

Memories, northern memories,
Bitter-stinging white world that bore us
Subsiding into this night.

Call it moonrise
This red anathema?

Rise, thou red thing,
Unfold slowly upwards, blood-dark;
Burst the night's membrane of tranquil stars
Finally.

Maculate
The red Macula.

D. H. Lawrence

A Night Sky (1916)

The moon, beyond her violet bars,
From towering heights of thunder-cloud,
Sheds calm upon our scarlet wars,
To soothe a world so small, so loud.
And little clouds like feathered spray,
Like rounded waves on summer seas,
Or frosted panes on a winter day,
Float in the dark blue silences.
Within their foam, transparent, white,
Like flashing fish the stars go by
Without a sound across the night.
In quietude and secrecy
The white, soft lightnings feel their way
To the boundless dark and back again,
With less stir than a gnat makes
In its little joy, its little pain.

Mary Webb

Dream Flight

When night begins to fall
I watch the sky until it's velvet dark
and suddenly I know I must step out –
the stars are strong enough to hold me now
and I'm foot-footing it
heel-to-toe, star to star
like hop-scotch in the sky.

I pass the moon and find that I – hello –
am interrupting midnight conversations
from satellites back down to mobile phones.
I overtake a rocket and surprise
sleepy astronauts on their way to Mars.

I wave and entertain them, juggling stars
back and forth, hand to hand
then leave them to rub their eyes
as I run up the Milky Way
into a game of chasing and I'm dancing, tumbling
with dreaming girls and boys across the sky.

As night goes on our dance turns into song
and I turn back and join the birds at dawn
singing in their chorus
as I flap my way
        back down
                to earth.

Lucinda Jacob

The Cat and the Moon

The cat went here and there
And the moon spun round like a top,
And the nearest kin of the moon,
The creeping cat, looked up.
Black Minnaloushe stared at the moon,
For, wander and wail as he would,
The pure cold light in the sky
Troubled his animal blood.
Minnaloushe runs in the grass
Lifting his delicate feet.
Do you dance, Minnaloushe, do you dance?
When two close kindred meet,
What better than call a dance?
Maybe the moon may learn,
Tired of that courtly fashion,
A new dance turn.
Minnaloushe creeps through the grass
From moonlit place to place,
The sacred moon overhead
Has taken a new phase.

Does Minnaloushe know that his pupils
Will pass from change to change,
And that from round to crescent,
From crescent to round they range?
Minnaloushe creeps through the grass
Alone, important and wise,
And lifts to the changing moon
His changing eyes.

W. B. Yeats

Wind and Silver

Greatly shining,
The Autumn moon floats in the thin sky;
And the fish-ponds shake their backs and flash
   their dragon scales
As she passes over them.

Amy Lowell

Of the Moon

Look how the pale queen of the silent night
Doth cause the Ocean to attend upon her,
And he, as long as she is in his sight,
With his full tide is ready her to honour;
But when the silver waggon of the Moon
Is mounted up so high he cannot follow,
The sea calls home his crystal waves to moan,
And with low ebb doth manifest his sorrow.
So you, that are the sovreign of my heart,
Have all my joys attending on your will,
My joys low-ebbing when you do depart –
When you return, their tide my heart doth fill:
So as you come, and as you do depart,
Joys ebb and flow within my tender heart.

Charles Best

Moon

you

spume-thrower

wave-stretcher

foam-snatcher

spray-raiser

surf-slinger

string-puller

scene-shifter

tide-turner

moon

Sue Cowling

The Witness

I am the silence,
The gesture of night;
The warden of darkness,
the bringer of light.

I have kept watch
Since the dawning of days:
The rising and setting;
The freeze and the haze.

I have observed
as you crept from the seas,
as you took your first breath,
as you stepped from the trees.

I kept my vigil
when you fell to your dreaming,
when you captured the flame,
when you made metal, gleaming.

I have borne witness
to your anger and hate,
your petty ambition,
your imperfect fate.

I have gazed down
As you smothered the land,
As you hacked at the forests,
As you turned fields to sand.

But there is no judgement:
My feelings are cold.
I shall still watch
When your world has grown old.

J. H. Rice

At a Lunar Eclipse

Thy shadow, Earth, from Pole to Central Sea,
Now steals along upon the Moon's meek shine
In even monochrome and curving line
Of imperturbable serenity.

How shall I link such sun-cast symmetry
With the torn troubled form I know as thine,
That profile, placid as a brow divine,
With continents of moil and misery?

And can immense Mortality but throw
So small a shade, and Heaven's high human scheme
Be hemmed within the coasts yon arc implies?

Is such the stellar gauge of earthly show,
Nation at war with nation, brains that teem,
Heroes, and women fairer than the skies?

Thomas Hardy

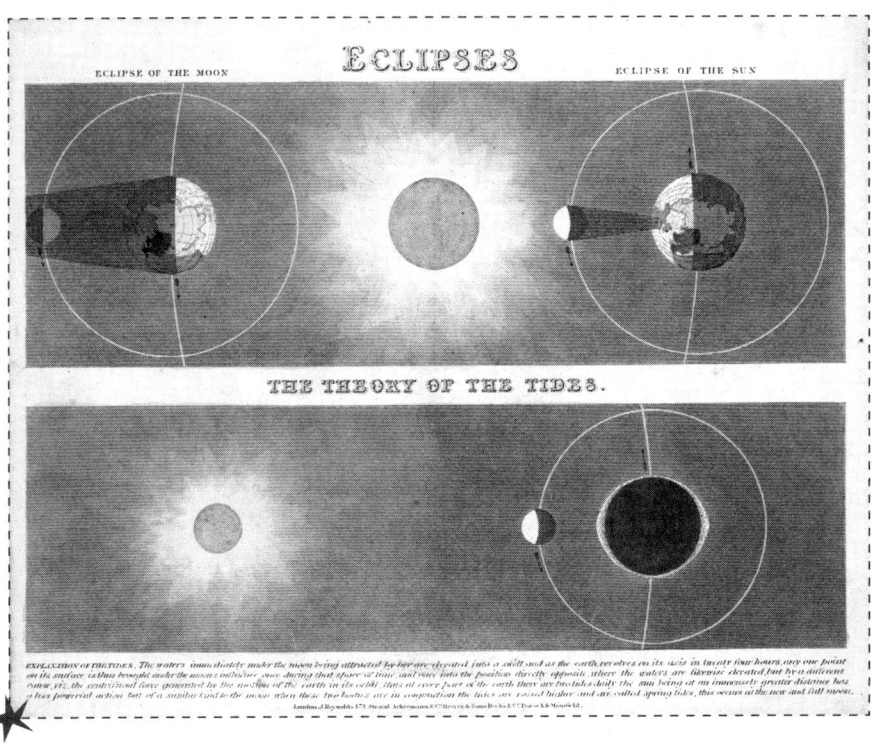

One of a set of twelve astronomical prints first issued in 1846.
This print shows eclipses and the theory of the tides.

On the Eclipse of the Moon of October 1865

One little noise of life remained – I heard
The train pause in the distance, then rush by,
Brawling and hushing, like some busy fly
That murmurs and then settles; nothing stirred
Beside. The shadow of our travelling earth
Hung on the silver moon, which mutely went
Through that grand process, without token sent,
Or any sign to call a gazer forth,
Had I not chanced to see: dumb was the vault
Of heaven, and dumb the fields – no zephyr swept
The forest walks, or through the coppice crept;
Nor other sound the stillness did assault,
Save that faint-brawling railway's move and halt;
So perfect was the silence Nature kept.

Charles Tennyson Turner

What Am I?

Earth orbiter
Rock blaster
Hook scraper
Shape caster

Sea puller
Night lighter
Sky watcher
Sun biter

Footprint hoarder
Flag carrier
Shadow sweeper
Meteor barrier

What am I?

Dom Conlon

The First Man in Space

Circling the earth
in an orbital spaceship,
he marvelled at the splendour
of our planet, saw
for the first time
its shape,
the folds of the terrain,
the shores of continents,
islands and great rivers
as well as large bodies of water.
It was, he declared
on his return,
a beauty
for the people of the world
to safeguard and enhance,
not destroy.
For the feelings which had filled him
as he flew
just a few miles up into the sky,
he could express with but one word —
'joy'.

Graham Denton

On 12 April 1961, 27-year-old Soviet Cosmonaut Flight Major Yuri Gagarin became the first human to journey into outer space when his Vostok 1 spacecraft completed an orbit of Earth. His flight lasted 108 minutes at a speed of 27,400 km/h.

The Loneliness of the Solo Astronaut

A world of worlds away
Silence echoes in my helmet
And I dream of voices
Messages from home

I can hear my every breath
The beating of my heart
Even the blood in my veins
Sounds like a rushing river

Just me and the stars
A mere speck in the firmament
Insignificant in the vastness
Wish you were here

Paul Cookson

Michael Collins

airforce pilot
flying higher, faster
from earth to atmosphere
through
and up
and on.

In a pressure suit
heavy with protections
jointed against its will

Mike travelled further
than all but two –
and then

trod water
in the dark/not-dark

watching the Moon
and waiting.

'I am alone now, truly alone'

14 orbits, solo
14 circuits of the Moon
21.5 hours

Every time he travelled
to the dark side of the Moon
absolute solitude

48 minutes
waiting
for Columbia to clear

slip round the cold rock
and return to radio contact
with the moonwalkers.

Capsule communicator
linchpin
between the ones who marked the lunar dust
and the anxious listeners on the blue planet,
waiting

for the voices to return

Imogen Russell Williams

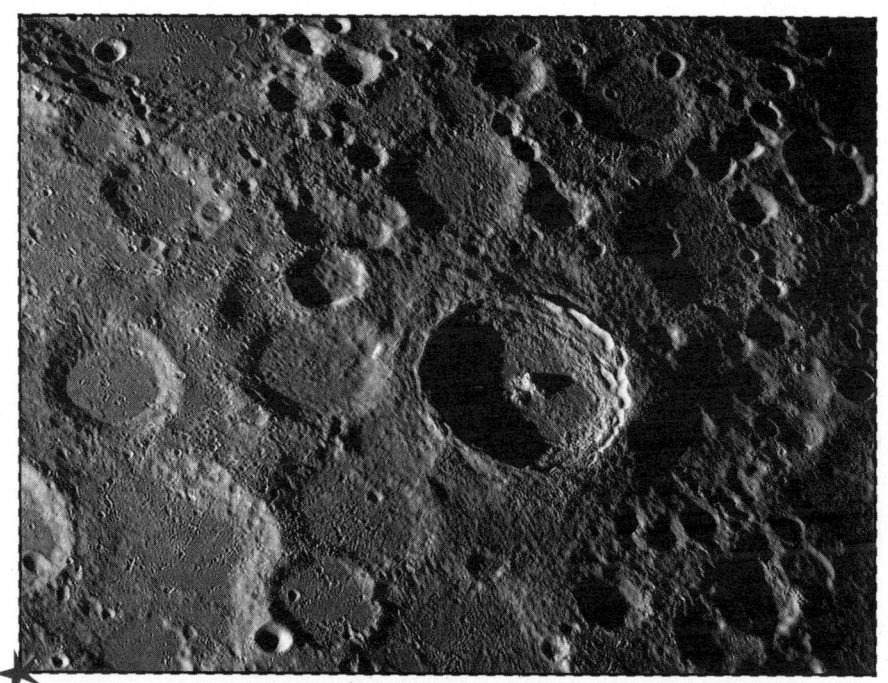

Photograph of the Moon's Tycho crater by George Tarsoudis, 2013

The Lonely Side of the Moon

Billions
(plus two)
on the other
side. But over
here, it's just   me
and radio
silence.

Laura Mucha

When Neil Armstrong and Buzz Aldrin launched towards the Moon in Apollo 11, it was Michael Collins' job to meet them afterwards.

As he swept behind the Moon, it blocked all radio transmissions to and from mission control – so for forty-eight minutes, Collins travelled in radio silence, separated from Planet Earth by 250,000 miles of space and the pile of broken bedrock, charcoal-grey, powdery dust and rocky debris we call the Moon.

On their return to Earth, Armstrong and Aldrin became household names, while Collins remained (relatively) anonymous.

Postcard from Space

A wondrous, fragile
marbled sphere
surrounded by
its atmosphere.
Deep white-wisped blue
with just a smear
of vibrant green,
then browns appear
as swirling curls
of cloud drift clear.
Breathtaking beauty –
wish you were here.

Jacqueline Shirtliff

*The Earthrise photo, taken in 1968 by the crew on board Apollo 8,
captured the first view of Earth from lunar orbit.*

Looking Back

Back slaps,
crawl in.
Straps.
Listen
to the rocket's
pops and cracks.
Notes from loved ones.
Close the hatch.

Light the engines.
Ship erupts.
All alone now,
pummelled,
crushed.

Unload rockets,
engines off,
eight, nine minutes
since taking off.
Weightless,
looking back at Earth,
our teeny, fragile
place of birth.

Home to us,
the human race,
a tiny part
of dark,
vast space.

Laura Mucha

This Rock, That Rock

This rock is big
That rock is small

This rock is blue
That rock is grey

This rock has trees
That rock has . . . rocks

This rock has rainbows
That rock has shadows

This rock has seasons
That rock does not

This rock has oceans of water
That rock has seas of dust

This rock is wrapped in a blue sky
That rock is loose within a black void

This rock orbits that sun
That rock orbits this rock

This rock is loud with stories and songs
That rock is as silent as a full stop

This rock has mountains filled with wealth
That rock has craters made poor by meteors

This rock is home to seven billion lives as brief as
    footprints in sand
That rock is home to footprints as long lasting as history

This rock is a planet
That rock is a moon

This rock is overflowing with life
That rock is what makes life on this rock possible

Dom Conlon

Universe

Let There Always Be Light
(Searching for Dark Matter)

For this we go out dark nights, searching
For the dimmest stars,
For signs of unseen things:

To weigh us down.
To stop the universe
From rushing on and on
Into its own beyond
Till it exhausts itself and lies down cold,
Its last star going out.

Whatever they turn out to be,
Let there be swarms of them,
Enough for immortality,
Always a star where we can warm ourselves.

Let there even be enough to bring it back
From its own edges,
To bring us all so close that we ignite
The bright spark of resurrection.

Rebecca Elson

Big Bang

In one intense instant
the universe went
from incredible density
to unending immensity

John Dougherty

We Used to Think the Universe Was Made . . .

We used to think the universe was made
of tiny invisible pin-points of energy, jostling
and tumbling and buzzing together, and so,
by whatever particular arrangement they took,
and the way in which they bounced off one another,
all sorts of physical matter could be produced.
Later we found the universe, in actual fact, is made
of tiny invisible threads of incredible length, and,

in the same way a violin string changes pitch
when touched at points along its measured span,
so all these interweaving loops and knots,
this tangle of quantum spaghetti,
as it flexes and line crosses line,
so it resonates throughout the whole bundle
a complex vibratory code that defines
any outward appearance and characteristic.

After which we discovered the likely reality
was of tiny invisible sheets, many layers
of infinitesimal thinness, each film
undulating at tremendous speeds;
multiple parallel oceans, their rippling surfaces
folding and flattening, wave-crests on wave-crests,
nudged at and nosed at, their lingering kisses
collected, expressed as specific material forms.

We were young, we were anxious to clutch at
whatever proof fitted. Still, humility liberates;
when it comes to matters of truth we're not picky.
Ironing our numbers presented the ideal
of tiny invisible shapeshifting blocks that squirm
and bulge, interlock and uncouple, that rub,
knock, wobble, split, and so make up
the whole gamut of substances we take for granted.

All this was long ago. Our models had risen
to eleven-dimensional-space when
our application for further funding was rejected
and we were asked to vacate the premises.
We took it well, were optimistic for the future,
though that was hardly the crux of the issue:
just try transporting eleven-dimensional furniture
in an incontrovertibly three-dimensional van.

J. O. Morgan

The Point

Point to the sky.
Draw a line from your finger.
It'll go on forever.
Through light and through darkness.
Past astronauts sleeping.
Past clouds and past planets.
Through silence unmeasured.
Through time uncounted.
A line that's so long.
It will never stop going.
Long after you've dropped
your hand to your side.
And gone back indoors.
That line is still sketching.
Onwards and outwards.
Universe threading.
Oh, your finger's a marvel.
Take care where you point it.

A. F. Harrold

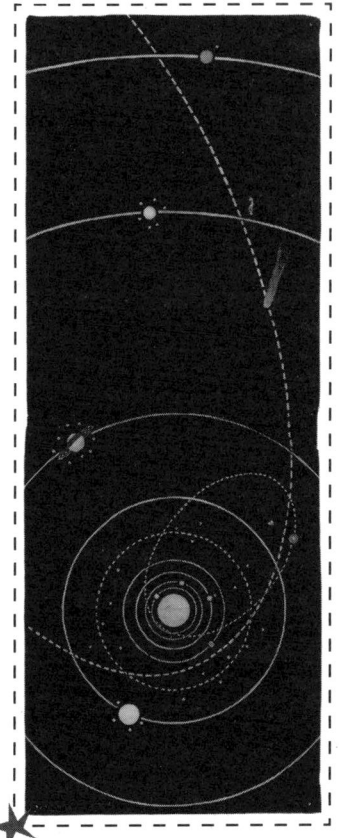

A cotton wall hanging from
the 1850s, showing the
solar system and planetary
orbits, including that of
Neptune, only discovered
in 1846

On Foot I Wandered Through the Solar Systems

On foot
I wandered through the solar systems,
before I found the first thread of my red dress.
Already I have a sense of myself.
Somewhere in space my heart hangs,
emitting sparks, shaking the air,
to other immeasurable hearts.

Edith Södergran
Translated by Malena Mörling and Jonas Ellerström

The Expanding Universe

How do they know, he is asking,
He is seven, maybe,
I am telling him how light
Comes to us like water,
Long red waves across the universe,
Everything, all of us,
Flying out from our origins.

And he is listening
As if I were not there,
Then walking back
Into the shadow of the chestnut,
Collecting pink blossoms
In his father's empty shoe.

Rebecca Elson

Relativity

for Stephen Hawking

When we wake up brushed by panic in the dark
our pupils grope for the shape of things we know.

Photons loosed from slits like greyhounds at the track
reveal light's doubleness in their cast shadows

that stripe a dimmed lab's wall – particles no more –
and with a wave bid all certainties goodbye.

For what's sure in a universe that dopplers
away like a siren's midnight cry? They say

a flash seen from on and off a hurtling train
will explain why time dilates like a perfect

afternoon; predicts black holes where parallel lines
will meet, whose stark horizon even starlight,

bent in its tracks, can't resist. If we can think
this far, might not our eyes adjust to the dark?

Sarah Howe

Planets of Our Solar System, Named in Order from the Sun

Mercury, Venus, Earth, Mars, Jupiter, Saturn, Uranus, Neptune

How do I remember those eight names?
Should I write them on the back of my hands?
    many very easy muses just speed up naming

But how do I learn their order from the sun?
Could I label lemons and lay them in a line?
    mighty velvet ears make jackrabbits sit up nicely

What if I muddle this planet with that?
What do I do if my mind goes blank?
    mucky vampires eating make jammy stains upon napkins

How can I remember when I have forgotten,
which planets are in our solar system?
    monkeys value every marvellous job sucking up nuts

There must be a way, when I go to bed,
to memorize the planets orbiting my head.
    merry vocal elephants murmur jolly songs until nighttime

Mandy Coe

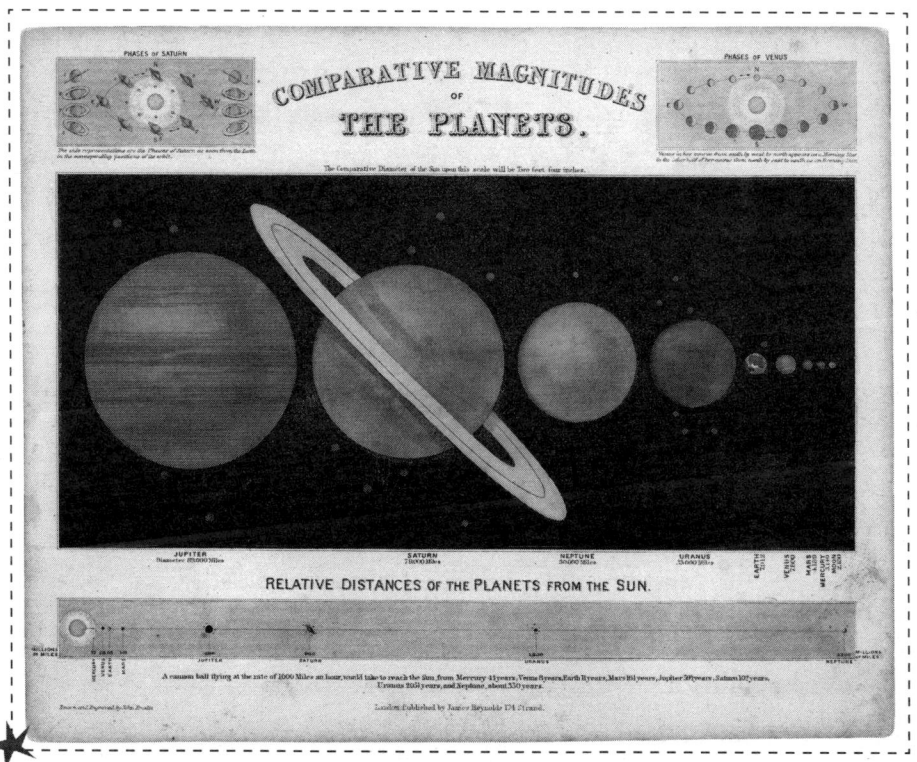

One of a set of twelve astronomical prints first issued in 1846.
This one shows the comparative sizes of the planets.

Aphelion

Aphelion
is when we're gone
as far as orbit takes us from
the power of the white-hot sun
whose pull, of course, is never done:
it beats its fearsome flaming drum
and back – elliptically – we come
until, once more, we run along
and happen on
aphelion.

Rachel Piercey

A Quark in the Dark

When I feel small, I think about a quark.
A quark is infinitely tiny.
Smaller than an ant.
Smaller than a full stop.
Smaller than a sand grain.
A million quarks will fit into one grain of sand.
To a quark, the sand grain is as big as our cities
of streets, houses, parks and sandpits.
This sand on my spade is an entire world to a quark.
I am a whole universe! One that the quark cannot
    understand.
When I feel small, I think about the vast and
    cosmic universe.
With glittering galaxies, hazy nebulas and
shimmering stars. And a tiny quark, in the dark.

Gita Ralleigh

Light Years

flicker by:
when green buds burst down Farm Lane
into petalled-flames;
goldfinches speckle hedgerows;
the breeze tickles trees,
and shames shadows
as easy sunlight claims space;
the earth sighs,
opens baby Arthur's hopeful eyes
as smiles crease a stranger's face.

But what about the heavy years?
Weeks stuck on overload
when each day is a surly weight?
Days when the light unravels
and seeps into darker places.

Light travels so fast
but distances between stars
and humans are vast –
so light takes its time,
slides across space
before we catch a night-time glimpse.

From the Milky Way's heart
where dark dust gathers between star-glitter,
a single glint of history reaches out,
aglow from 26,000 years ago.

Pie Corbett

A light year is the distance light travels in one year –
almost 6 trillion miles!

Space is Silent

No one can hear you scream
in space

because there's nothing to vibrate
carrying a voice from
mouth to ear –

even explosions
are puffed-out paper bags
too soft to burst
damp squibs.

Big Bang? Blast of *silence*:
tight hot hush
sprayed into a hair-mousse universe.

Assassin stars are shooting with the silencers on.

There are no noisy parties.
The music of the spheres
is muted
(by complaints
from the neighbourhood's peevish moons).

And yet
not all of space is vacuum.

There is some sound out there.

Asteroids patter   fragments
meteors hiss   in radio waves
black holes   *sing*

Perhaps
with bigger
sharper
attuned ears

swivelling like elephants'
live satellite dishes

we might hear

different screams

Imogen Russell Williams

Space

a spatter
toothbrush dipped
a bristle-flick
of luminous milk

Space

a crust
of diamond dust
on velvet black
and billowed silk

Space

a mirror
for our stories

Space

a vacuum
for our junk

Space

frontier
event horizon

Space
>   grey bulkhead
>   suit   seat   bunk

Space
>   the place
>   creation happens

Space
>   remote
>   and close at hand

Space
>   a teacup
>   of tornadoes

Space
>   stars flung
>   like grains of sand

Space
>   a cradle
>   and a ladle
>   bow and serpent
>   cross and bear

Space

    a grave
    for light
    that trails
    from stars
    that are
    no longer
    there

Imogen Russell Williams

Impossible Things

Sometimes
When things seem impossible
Or if you feel as if you don't fit in
Just remember that on Mars the sunsets are blue
    and Venus spins backwards
        and that far out in our galaxy
           there is a planet with a heart of
           diamonds
Remind yourself that one teaspoon of a neutron star
Weighs more than all the humans on our planet put
    together
Know that some rogue planets
    just wander the galaxy
        completely alone
And some planets are speeding away from us so fast
That we will never see them
In fact, in the immeasurable vastness of space
    There is no such thing
        As a typical planetary system
        Or a typical planet
           Because each one is unique
           Just like you

Dawn McLachlan

Brief Interview with a Gravitationally Completely Collapsed Object

Many thanks for agreeing to this interview.
I have so many questions to ask you.
I wonder, are there other names you go by?

Oh sure, I've been called many things; a void
nothingness, empty space, oblivion, chasm, abyss.
I prefer Supernova, it's what I used to be.

That's a cool name, what happened?
Didn't you use to be a big star? Massive, right?
Some said you were bigger than the sun!

I guess I just got too big for myself. Gravity
got the better of me, and I ran out of fuel.
But I tell you, I went out with a bang!

Well, you certainly caused an explosion.
The whole world was absorbed. And then
nothing. Can you shed light on the matter?

I'm as in the dark as you are. Attraction is
a mysterious thing. Who knows what works
as a draw, but it's the only proof of my existence.

Relationships are complicated, aren't they?
That's another black hole. Final question. How
close are you to . . . Hello? Hello? Still there?

Void, nothingness, empty space, oblivion, chasm, abyss

Cheryl Moskowitz

Supernova

I am brought
by gravity
and galaxies
by light,
over distance
imagination
cannot size;
you see me
maybe –
maybe again,
as I journey
until the
longest path
I take arrives,
when all
the intervening
space aligns.

I was a star,
I shone.
Now my stardust
slowly follows
on and on,
and when my
dust is come,
maybe you, too,
will be gone.

Liz Brownlee

The Water in the Glass You are Holding Right Now*

has led a million lives.
It has survived.

Perhaps a splash or two
dashed once or twice
across Niagara Falls.

Or lay locked in the ice
of the first snowball you threw.

Or you'll discover
this water once washed the hands of your
great-great-great grandmother.

Maybe it powered the leaves
of your favourite tree.

Or once was brewed as tea
or (forgive me)
kangaroo wee.

* (Feel free to fetch one.)

Perhaps it held the drops
that quenched the thirst
of the very first
triceratops.

Water goes nowhere and everywhere.
Water knows everything.

So it's not such a leap
to think
you hold in your hand
a link
to every kind of wildness,
to every kind of person.

Drink deep.

Kate Wakeling

Some scientists believe that all the water we have on Earth arrived around 3.8 billion years ago, delivered by a series of icy space rocks that came hurtling through the solar system and onto our planet, in an event known as the 'Late Heavy Bombardment'.

The History of Nothing

'Once there was nothing,
then a pebble of gas and dust,
rock and atoms plus swirling,
fantastic energies all exploded
in a Big Bang!' said our teacher.

'My brain hurts,' whispered Sanjay.

'It made the universe,
which stretched and expanded,
growing bigger and bigger, creating
stars and suns, moons and planets,
like our planet Earth,' said our teacher.

'And dinosaurs?' asked Sanjay.

'Yes and humans later on
and oxygen, carbon dioxide, oceans,
clouds, skies and it didn't stop. It's still spinning
outwards, making black holes, new nebulae
and galaxies,' said our teacher.

'And aliens?' laughed Sanjay.

'Don't know about that,
Sanjay but thank you for asking.
And there was nothing at all there before
this explosion, just empty darkness
going on forever,' said our teacher.

'What's nothing? asked Sanjay.

'Ten minus ten,' smiled Clever Chloe.
'But there must have been something
you can't just have nothing. Nothing is a Something
if that's all there is,' said Sanjay.
'Well there was nothing,' said our teacher.

'Now is that the bell?'

'I think they make this stuff up
to confuse us, even if it's true,' I said
on the yard but Sanjay wasn't listening,
he was playing football with Smigsy
so I went in goal.

And we won, five nothing.

David Harmer

Aurora Borealis

An aurora borealis,
also called the Northern Lights,
is a natural phenomenon
on pitch-black, cloudless nights.

This surreal auroral curtain
has a neon greenish glow.
One of seven natural wonders –
it's our planet's finest show.

Darren Sardelli

A Whole Universe

you're a whole universe
vast and unknowable space
expanding every day

you're the unfolding
of countless dreams
hopes and ideas
a quiet creative power
bringing new galaxies
into being

magnificent just the way you are
you're chaos, beautiful chaos
and nothing can stop you

Rashmi Sirdeshpande

We Have Space Dust in Our Hair

What does it mean to be human?
One heart?
One brain?
An opposable thumb?
Words on our tongues?
Love?

Or is it travel to places we can't even see?
Is it the taste of an apple in space?
Is it a telescope one million miles away, beaming
    images to Earth?
Is it the fact that those amazing stars outnumber us
    and we can't help but stare?
Or
Is it having space dust in our hair?
And learning, knowing, *proving* it is there?

Attie Lime

Shades of Shooting Star

Soar
We'll watch you
All aflame with
Elements

Blaze
Your violet calcium
Your orange sodium
Your red, red oxygen

Dazzle
Vibrant sky-colours
Burn us a brand-new
Rainbow

Attie Lime

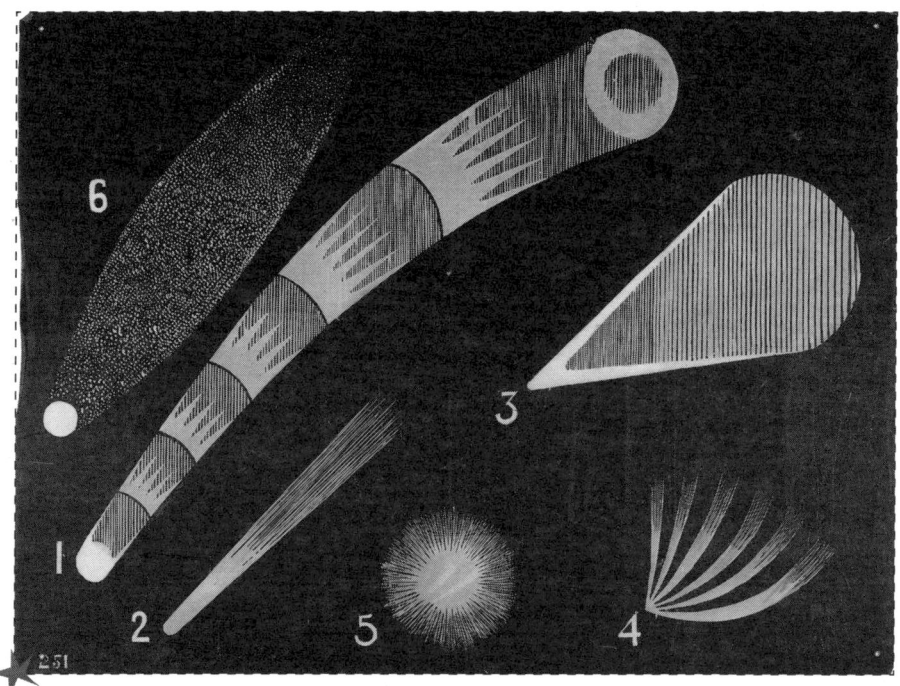

An 1850s cotton wall hanging showing six comets, among which is Halley's Comet, numbered 3

The Perseids

standing here,
looking up
as a thousand stars
dance across
the night sky,
for a moment,
the universe
feels so big
and my worries
so very small.

Rashmi Sirdeshpande

It Hurtled Down to Middlesbrough

I once held a meteorite
in the palm of my hand
the size of my hand

It hurtled down to Middlesbrough
on the 14th March 1881
still flying at
281 miles per hour
stopped by a buffer of soil

when they reached inside the hole
to take it out
it was
as warm as a handshake

And I held that meteorite
in the palm of my hand
a 24-year-old hand
holding something
4.5 billion years old

as old as the Earth
unchanged
wandering in space
until
it hurtled down to Middlesbrough

Myles McLeod

A print of the meteor seen from Paddington, London by
Matthew Cotes Wyatt, 11 February 1850

The International Space Station Above Our House

A wash of navy-blue night is being winched up in the
    east;
a dwindling day is toppling into the hill in the west.

Our neighbours gather in this September silence;
the children are excited, the adults are bemused by
    my invite.

A dozen questions are fired – how high, what size,
    who's in it?
I should have the answers, but I know few facts – just
    the poetry of it.

A speck of shy light high in the west; the enchantment
    begins
as the International Space Station glides gracefully
    into view.

The children scream in delight, the adults are smiling
    at the sky
as out of the lonely wings of the west and into centre
    stage

this silver-white machine tiptoes resolutely,
    metaphorically,
above us pointing to our future – our beloved,
    artificial angel.

John Rice

The Galaxy

Torrent of light and river of the air,
    Along whose bed the glimmering stars are seen
    Like gold and silver sands in some ravine
    Where mountain streams have left their
        channels bare!
The Spaniard sees in thee the pathway, where
    His patron saint descended in the sheen
    Of his celestial armor, on serene
    And quiet nights, when all the heavens were fair.
Not this I see, nor yet the ancient fable
    Of Phaeton's wild course, that scorched the skies
    Where'er the hoofs of his hot coursers trod;
But the white drift of worlds o'er chasms of sable,
    The star-dust that is whirled aloft and flies
    From the invisible chariot-wheels of God.

Henry Wadsworth Longfellow

Comet

(To be read as quickly as possible, in as few breaths as you can manage.)

I'm a spinning, winning, tripping, zipping, super-sonic
    ice queen:
see my moon zoom, clock my rocket, watch me splutter
    tricksy space-steam.

I'm the dust bomb, I'm the freeze sneeze, I'm the top
    galactic jockey
made (they think) of gas and ice and mystery bits of
    something rocky.

Oh I sting a sherbet orbit, running rings round star or
    planet;
should I shoot too near the sun, my tail hots up: *ouch –*
    OUCH – please fan it!

And I'm told I hold the answer to the galaxy's top question:
that my middle's made of history (no surprise I've
    indigestion)

but for now I sprint and skid and whisk and bolt and
    belt and bomb it;
I'm that hell-for leather, lunging, plunging, helter-
    skelter COMET.

Kate Wakeling

To Halley's Comet

Thou 'Wanderer' out in the vast Unknown,
　　When next upon thy path around the sun
　　Thou dost return, how many will have run
Their race who saw thee last, and youth have grown
To age, and many changes will be here!
　　Such progress has the mind of man achieved
　　In knowledge of the heavens, 'tis scarce believed;
Yet more 'twill know when next thou shalt appear.
While thou, returning, wilt thy path pursue
　　For centuries, and many millions will
　　Thy coming watch and recognize, until,
At last thou, too, shalt disappear from view;—
　　Worn out, dissolved, and scattered far through
　　　space,
　　No more shall men behold thee in thy place!

Alice Berlingett

A cartoon titled 'Searching for Halley's Comet at Greenwich Observatory', 1909

Halley's Comet

I am ice and carbon dust and silicate
Around the Galaxy I dance
Lighting up your planet's sky
In 240 BC in China
Someone recorded me passing by

In 12 BC the Romans say
I portended the death
of Marcus Vipsanius Agrippa
(I'm big on historical landmarks)
Some people claim
I was the Star of Bethlehem
But I think that's a bit far fetched

In 451 I heralded the defeat
of Attila the Hun
and in 1066 when William the Conqueror
Conquered
They said I was an omen in the sky
That foretold Harold would die
(Have you heard of the Bayeux Tapestry?
You'll find me there)

And then in 1696
Edmond Halley worked out
That all those comets blazing through the stars
Were one and the same
That's right – ME!
And that's how I got my name.

I was last here in 1986
And I'll be back in 2061, in July
See you then.
Bye.

Roger Stevens

Halley's Comet

Halley didn't live to see it
though he had worked out the date
from its previous visits
would be 1758.

The first known observation
was in 164 BC.
Its 1066 sighting is sewn
into the Bayeux Tapestry.

In *The Adoration of the Magi*
Giotto's Star of Bethlehem
may have been inspired
by it in 1301.

Shakespeare thought that comets
were heralds, coincidences.
In Julius Caesar the comet
'blazed forth the death of princes'.

The first photo of the comet
was caught in 1910.
On that occasion
it came closer than the sun.

In '86 an 'Armada'
moved in as it swept by;
mum's school got out the bunting
for this wonder in the sky.

Carole Bromley

Dazzle Dance

I am made of heat and light
comets spinning through the night
spit and splinter – meteorite
firecracker, pinwheel bright.

I am made from ash and coal
watch my embers wax and glow
twist and turn my body so
dragon breath to volcano.

I have frazzle crackle hands
dance a razzle dazzle dance
simmer swirling twist and prance
glitter, sparkle to entrance.

I am made of cinder stars
gasses burning from afar
supernova in the dark
flash of thunder full of spark.

I incinerate and blaze
candles burning in my gaze
born of fire, heat and flame
come and bask beneath my rays.

Sue Hardy-Dawson

Rosetta and the Singing Comet

I left the Earth
I hurtled high
I heard the comet's
distant sigh
I drank the sun
It gave me wings
I heard the comet
whirr and sing
I swung past Mars
its pair of moons
I heard the comet
hum a tune
A lullaby
for cold extremes
I heard the comet
in my dreams
And then I woke
drawn in and in
I danced in orbit
held to spin
I circled round
and round and round
The comet made
its secret sound
I told the humans

what I saw
The comet sang
I told them more
The comet took me
from the sun
We sailed towards
aphelion
My eyes were tired
My wings grew weak
I thought I heard
the comet speak
I leant in close
and closer still
I felt its wild
magnetic thrill
I fell through swirls
of gas and dust
I rushed towards
its icy crust
I heard the comet
say: Rosetta
Come to me
Let's sing together . . .

Rachel Piercey

Rosetta was a space probe investigating a comet called 67P/Churyumov-Gerasimenko. When Rosetta reached the comet after ten years of flight, it picked up a 'song' made of oscillations in the comet's magnetic field.

Hooligan Comets

Dirty snowballs
charged by solar
pluming up for two-tailed flight

peeling off
in gas and dust fumes
scrawling ionized blue light

pitted misfits
skewed elliptics
warped by planet gravity

bitten by hot
travel bug
won't settle into family

apparitions
stellar roaming
till they shed their hair at last

bald, sedate
long-travelled burnouts –
asteroids with colourful pasts

Imogen Russell Williams

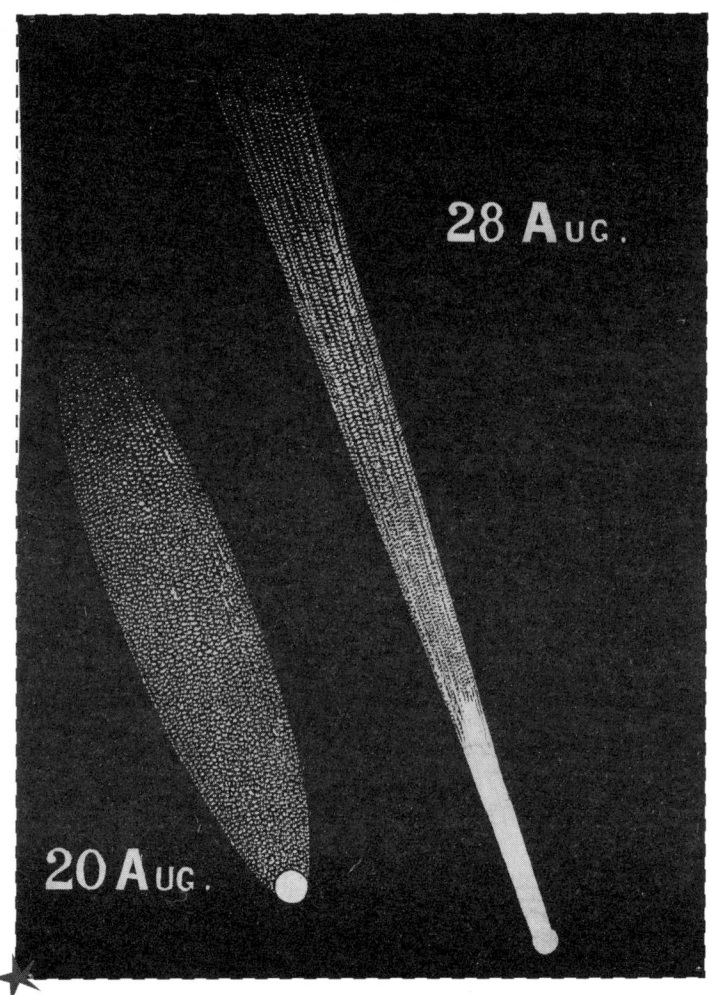

An 1850s cotton wall hanging showing two comets, both of which may be views of Donati's Comet from 1858

Bedtime Reading

This comet's tail is drawn in reflected light,
dip a stick in a pond and move it
left to right. The trail it leaves
is a story of origin and flight.

Comets, Hale-Bopp and Ikeya-Seki,
throw stones in the pond and watch ripples race.
Comets, Halle and Shoemaker-Levy,
their magnetic waves telling tales in space.

In the mountains and deserts, far from city lights,
the readers of the universe wake up
and rub their eyes. While we're in bed, they're busy
reading the trails and tales that fill the skies.

Mandy Coe

People

We Astronomers

We astronomers are nomads,
Merchants, circus people,
All the earth our tent.

We are industrious.
We breed enthusiasms,
Honour our responsibility to awe.

But the universe has moved a long way off.
Sometimes, I confess,
Starlight seems too sharp,

And like the moon
I bend my face to the ground,
To the small patch where each foot falls,

Before it falls,
And I forget to ask questions,
And only count things.

Rebecca Elson

When I Heard the Learn'd Astronomer

When I heard the learn'd astronomer,
When the proofs, the figures, were ranged in columns before me,
When I was shown the charts and diagrams, to add, divide, and measure them,
When I sitting heard the astronomer where he lectured with much applause in the lecture-room,
How soon unaccountable I became tired and sick,
Till rising and gliding out I wander'd off by myself,
In the mystical moist night-air, and from time to time,
Look'd up in perfect silence at the stars.

Walt Whitman

Three Hundred and Fifty Earth Years Ago . . .

Three hundred and fifty Earth years ago
What did an informed astronomer know?
They'd know that our moon reflected sunlight
As it circled the Earth in its orbital flight.
They'd know that Earth's satellite showed just one
side.
(And, maybe, they'd wonder what it had to hide?)
They'd think just five planets, as well as our own,
Elliptically circled our great, golden sun.
They'd have some idea of the distance between
The Earth, sun and moon and the planets they'd seen
But they too would think, for all their education,
That our solar system was all of creation.
Still, given the tools that they had in those days,
I think what they knew most deserving of praise.

Philip Waddell

The year 2025 will mark the 350th anniversary since the laying of the foundation stone for the Royal Observatory in Greenwich.

What Astronomers Know (or Think) in 2025

They know that the universe is very cold
And, nearly, they think, fourteen billion years old.
They think a Big Bang was space's derivation
And space is expanding through cosmic inflation.
They think that dark energy makes space expand
And think that dark matter they will understand.
And galaxies may, they think, number in trillions
With stars and with planets that number in billions.
Some think that, in time, we'll find we're not alone
So, SETI is seeking to solve this unknown.
Celestial ideas are picking up pace
But, still, there's so much to deduce about space
And more will be known but I'm sure there will be
Questions unanswered for all eternity.

Philip Waddell

*Space is extremely cold, barely above absolute zero which is −273.15°C,
although the temperature is not constant throughout the universe.
SETI stands for the Search for Extraterrestrial Intelligence.*

Galileo

Galileo,
an Italian guy,
built his own telescope,
studied the sky.
Examined the moon,
the Milky Way, Venus,
the rings around Saturn –
astronomical genius!

Caught sight of Jupiter's
four moons one night.
By Copernicus! I think
that fellow was right!
The Earth's not the centre
of all that exists;
I've proved it's the sun
that dwells in the midst!

The Church didn't like
the things that he said,
but that didn't stop him!
The new ideas spread.
Before very long
he was under arrest,
locked up in his house
and feeling quite stressed.

Can't you see that you're wrong!
his enemies cried.
He kept at his work
till the day that he died.
Four hundred years later
he's long dead and gone,
but we know he was right
and his name still lives on.

Jacqueline Shirtliff

In 1543, Copernicus said, 'In the midst of all dwells the Sun.'
He was the first person to state that Earth and the other planets
travel around the Sun.

Galileo (1564–1642)

I heard about the first telescope
being made in Holland – too far
away for me to see from Pisa,
but still, I made my own.
It was better.

I saw the mountains and valleys
of the moon, sunspots,
the four largest moons of Jupiter.

You might think you are the centre
of the universe,
and most people did,
but we revolve around the sun.

New ideas are hard to break.
I stuck to mine and was imprisoned.
First in jail, then in a villa
I could not leave.

Thought is slow to change.
I hold no grudge.
The truth will out

and in time I was named a father –
The Father of Modern Science.
Now my thoughts trip lightly
through the centuries.

Chrissie Gittins

Lithographic portrait of Galileo Galilei

Lithographic portrait of Nicolaus Copernicus

Copernicus Kicked Up a Fuss

Nicolaus Copernicus
Stared hard at the universe
Then told everyone
The Earth moves round the Sun.

Many important people said
The Sun moves round the Earth instead.
He said *It's a heliocentric system*
With moving planets, here I'll list them.

Round and round the Sun they go.
His enemies still shouted *NO!*
He was right but to be critical
His orbits were circular, not elliptical.

Johannes Kepler put matters right.
The Sun stands still all day and night
People can say 'That's Hocus-Pocus!'
But the Sun is always a planet's focus.

David Harmer

Expanding Forever

(Inspired by the astronomer, Beatrice Tinsley –
who proved the universe was expanding.)

I
began with a big bang
now there is no stopping
no slowing
no end or edge or limits
to my open endless growing

Only the redshift
of an infinite galactic elastic band
expanding forever
as I stretch away
from wherever you stand

For where you are
is always my centre

Elena de Roo

You Can't Just Point a Rocket at the Sky and Hope

You can't just point a rocket at the sky
and hope a passing moon will catch it.

You have to plan
and plot
work out which spot
to leave from
know the landing place
and where re-entry's going to happen.

You need to find the line
of flight
fine hone your calculations
speculations
will not do it
guesswork
only leads to messwork.

So whose great maths work
put the first men up in space?
Dozens of women
working out the numbers.

Before the world filled up with PCs
tablets, smartphones,
these women worked it out.

They did the maths
that took the human race
up into space.

Back then computers
had a human
female
face.

Jan Dean

Katherine Johnson, who worked at NASA, was one of the 'human computers' described in this poem. She called that era 'the time when computers wore a skirt'.

For All Mankind

When it comes to the history
of manned space flight
I'd like to mention
that the first men on the Moon
and many after that
were carried there
and helped there
and rescued there
and brought back from there
by women.

Like Margaret Hamilton
who wrote the code
to make Apollo fly
and not only that
but bring it back again.

Like Katherine Johnson
the mathematician who
calculated trajectories
making it possible
to orbit a planet.

Like Catherine Osgood
figuring out how to dock
in space – which enabled
the lunar module
to do its job.

Like Dorothy Vaughan
who taught herself
and others how to program,
helping to launch
rockets into space.

Like Mary Jackson
the first female black engineer
who became an expert
with wind tunnels
and inspiring others.

Like Jerrie Cobb
who taught men how to fly
and passed the tests
to be an astronaut
but was never sent to space.

Like these and all the women
seen and unseen
whose footprints
have been lost
so do yourself a favour:
when you start to think
of all those spacemen
of history
of manned spaceflight
to the Moon just
stop
think space-people
think our-story
think crewed,
and think how to be
humankind.

Dom Conlon

June 1963

Valentina smiles
> From Vostok 6 the world looks fragile
> somewhere down there the Volga flows
> her father drives his tractor
> and her mother's working in the cotton mill.

Valentina smiles
> Fills in her logbook
> checks the instruments.
> watches the lovely earth
> as she revolves in steady orbit.

Valentina smiles
> ALONE for three days
> circling and circling our planet.
> The sky is black and full of stars . . .

Valentina smiles.
> We watch her on TV,
> millions of us see that smile
> and wonder what she's thinking.

Valentina smiles
    She dreams of parachutes
    round as the domes of jellyfish
    of diving through the sky
    borne up by curved white silk.
    She falls in love with space
and smiles.

Jan Dean

Valentina Tereshkova was the first woman to fly in space. (She'd told her mother she was going on a parachute course when in fact she was going to orbit the Earth.) The most famous photograph of her shows her smiling.

Chaika

Chaika,
Valentina Tereshkova,
flew her Vostok module over
Earth in June of sixty-three. When
she launched, she said with glee, 'Hey
sky, take off your hat, I'm coming.' (Or
if you'd like your Russian true: 'Yey,
nyeba, snimi shlyapu, ya idoo.') And
so, the seagull soared, stargazing.
Three days, forty-eight orbits
later, she drove her rocket
back to vapour. Her dad had
driven tractors, later tanks. So
never saw his Vladimirovna
thanked with a Soviet outburst
for being the first woman in
space. Hero. Ace. Years later
missions to Mars are
mooted, and Valentina
says she'll be
booted,
suited.

And take a one-way cosmo-climb

to be the first a second time.

Myles McLeod

Chaika *is the Russian word for seagull and it was Tereshkova's radio call sign.*

The Old Astronomer

REACH me down my Tycho Brahé,—I would know
    him when we meet,
When I share my later science, sitting humbly at his feet;
He may know the law of all things, yet be ignorant of
    how
We are working to completion, working on from then
    till now.

Pray, remember, that I leave you all my theory
    complete,
Lacking only certain data, for your adding, as is meet;
And remember, men will scorn it, 'tis original and true,
And the obloquy of newness may fall bitterly on you.

But, my pupil, as my pupil you have learnt the worth
    of scorn;
You have laughed with me at pity, we have joyed to be
    forlorn;
What, for us, are all distractions of men's fellowship
    and smiles?
What, for us, the goddess Pleasure, with her
    meretricious wiles?

You may tell that German college that their honour
    comes too late.
But they must not waste repentance on the grizzly
    savant's fate;
Though my soul may set in darkness, it will rise in
    perfect light;
I have loved the stars too truly to be fearful of the night.

What, my boy, you are not weeping? You should save
    your eyes for sight;
You will need them, mine observer, yet for many
    another night.
I leave none but you, my pupil, unto whom my plans
    are known.
You 'have none but me,' you murmur, and I 'leave you
    quite alone'?

Well then, kiss me,—since my mother left her
    blessing on my brow,
There has been a something wanting in my nature
    until now;
I can dimly comprehend it,—that I might have been
    more kind,
Might have cherished you more wisely, as the one I
    leave behind.

I 'have never failed in kindness'? No, we lived too high
    for strife,—
Calmest coldness was the error which has crept into our
    life;
But your spirit is untainted, I can dedicate you still
To the service of our science: you will further it? you will!

There are certain calculations I should like to make with
    you,
To be sure that your deductions will be logical and true;
And remember, 'Patience, Patience,' is the watchword of
    a sage,
Not to-day nor yet to-morrow can complete a perfect age.

I have sown, like Tycho Brahé, that a greater man may reap;
But if none should do my reaping, 'twill disturb me in my
    sleep.
So be careful and be faithful, though, like me, you leave
    no name;
See, my boy, that nothing turn you to the mere pursuit
    of fame.

I must say Good-bye, my pupil, for I cannot longer
    speak;
Draw the curtain back for Venus, ere my vision grows
    too weak:
It is strange the pearly planet should look red as fiery
    Mars,—
God will mercifully guide me on my way amongst the
    stars.

Sarah Williams

Alfonso Churchill

They laughed at me as 'Prof. Moon,'
As a boy in Spoon River, born with the thirst
Of knowing about the stars.
They jeered when I spoke of the lunar mountains,
And the thrilling heat and cold,
And the ebon valleys by silver peaks,
And Spica quadrillions of miles away,
And the littleness of man.
But now that my grave is honored, friends,
Let it not be because I taught
The lore of the stars in Knox College,
But rather for this: that through the stars
I preached the greatness of man,
Who is none the less a part of the scheme of things
For the distance of Spica or the Spiral Nebulae;
Nor any the less a part of the question
Of what the drama means.

Edgar Lee Masters

First Lady of the Stars

'The eyes of her who is glorified here below turned to the starry heavens.' (Caroline Herschel's tombstone)

Who would have thought that a lady astronomer
in the distant eighteenth century
was a full-blown, professional star-gazer,
while living demurely and gently?

Caroline Lucretia Herschel
to give you the lady's full name
worked with her brother, William,
although he got more of the fame.

By day Caroline polished the lenses
and made the refractors bright.
At dusk, she set up her telescope
and studied the planets at night.

And what do you think she discovered
back in the days of yore? –
fourteen deep-sky objects,
eight comets and much more.

She was honoured by the Royal Society
– (highly unusual then),
for astronomers and philosophers
were all of them distinguished MEN.

So, to all you scientist girls,
being female is no bar;
Herschel's skills in tracking comets
made her a rising star!

Jane Newberry

Caroline Herschel, 1750–1848. Awesome lady – go on, Google her.

Caroline Herschel
From an oil painting by Tielemann 1829
In the possession of Sir W. J. Herschel, Bart.

A portrait of Caroline Herschel after a
painting by Professor Tielemann, 1829

What Caroline Herschel Remembers

I remember sweeping floors in Hanover,
scrubbing copper pans, mending endless shirts,
wondering if my life would ever change.

I remember worrying if my scarred face, my blind eye,
my height of only four foot three
would stop me making something of my life.

I remember shrivelling up inside
when my mother said she didn't believe
in daughters being educated.

I remember my brother William sending money from
  Bath
so my mother could employ a servant to replace me.
The honey-coloured stone of that city made my heart
  sing.

I remember my brother taught me mathematics.
At night we would look out at the sky
and talk of our father's love of the stars.

I remember on clear nights William would look through
the telescope and I'd note down his measurements
of objects in the sky. The ink froze in my inkwell.

I remember the telescopes we made
needed a cheap material for the mirror moulds.
Dried and powdered horse dung did the trick.

I remember when William was away I took a look
through the telescope for myself. My heart burst
like a spurting firework when I saw a new glow of
   glittering light.

I remember thinking, 'Is it a star or could it be a comet?'
It was in a place a star shouldn't be; to prove it was a
   comet
I had to show it moved from one night to the next.

I remember my trepidation the next day when it rained
and the clouds hung low. Would I be able to see
the gleaming light that night?

I remember the clouds parting and there it was
winking back at me from a different position.
It *was* a comet! We beamed together.

I remember King George III was so impressed when
   he saw it
he gave me a salary of fifty pounds a year.
And so I became the first female astronomer to be paid.

I remember making many more discoveries –
seven more comets, fourteen new nebulae –
I improved a catalogue by adding five hundred extra
    stars.

I remember being given gold medals and
membership of important institutions.
I believe there is even a Google Doodle.

But I never forgot that I went from sweeping floors
to sweeping the skies, from being invisible
to becoming – you could say – a comet-like shining light.

Chrissie Gittins

*Caroline Herschel (1750–1848) was a pioneering astronomer. An asteroid,
star clusters and a satellite have been named after her. Her achievements have
encouraged generations of women to develop a career in the sciences. Until the
1980s, she held the record for the most comets discovered by a woman.*

Census Taker of the Sky

She was a girl stargazer,
was Annie Jump Cannon, was she.
Gifted down from mother to daughter,
a love of the heavens, you see.

Each night she looked at pictures
in the astronomy book by her bed.
The pages lit dimly by candle
struck dreams in the little girl's head.

The stars she saw in the drawings,
matched with those in the night sky outside.
'I won't rest until they're all counted!'
from the attic window she cried.

A fever captured her hearing,
but it was stars that captured her heart.
Annie announced she was *Astronomer*,
true scientist right from the start.

She taught herself photography,
studied measurement, physics and maths.
Became chief amongst 'Pickering's Women' –
their job to accumulate facts.

Now stars have classifications,
and a way of remembering them.
Oh, Be A Fine Girl – Kiss Me! Annie's rhyme
for O, B, A, F, G, K, M.

Charting stars from hottest to coolest,
Annie Jump Cannon made history.
Proof that to be a star girl stargazer
is the coolest star you can be!

Cheryl Moskowitz

Annie Maunder Explains the Sun

* Sun spots migrate like whales
    wandering across the ocean of the sun

* The sun's corona is a lion's mane here,
    a dandelion's windswept crown there

* Sun spots are pimples breaking on the sun's face
    caused by mighty feelings held inside

* A child pulls off the sun's petals in an eclipse
    calling *Loves me, Loves me not*

* You may pepper your fried egg with sun spots
    break its yolk like a coronal flare

* Sun spots pass across the page
    like well-behaved butterflies in flight

* Sometimes the sun streaks
    like a laughing lady across a cricket pitch

Anna Kisby

Some of these Sun descriptions are in Annie Maunder's own words, from her book The Heavens and their Story *(1908); some are inspired by Annie's solar photographs.*

The Lady Computers

(1890–1895)

That's what their bosses called them,
those fresh-faced mathematicians
with galaxies in their gaze;
Edith and Isabella,
Harriet and young Alice,
spinning webs of figures round
stars, with the delicate touch
of celestial watchmakers
trapping slow, refracted time.
Files now lost in some black hole,
these astrographic pioneers,
these foragers of vital facts,
are long-forgotten relics
of days when women's work just
didn't matter quite enough.

Lucy Coats

*I have used some of Isabella Clemes' own words in this poem,
taken from her 1891 article in* The Churchman.

Cecilia

She discovered what the universe was made of
despite the obstacles the world set in her way.

They allowed her to study, to earn a degree
but not to receive it
because she was a woman.

She moved abroad to study the stars
to observe them, calculate their composition
and, doing so
she discovered what the universe was made of.

But the important man who reviewed her work
told her she was wrong
told her she would damage her career
if she went against the consensus

so she disavowed her own discovery
because she was a woman.

Four years later, the important man
discovered she was right
published his own work
was given the credit.

But she was the one
who realized the stars were made of hydrogen

who discovered what the universe was made of.

Remember her name:
Cecilia Payne

John Dougherty

Cecilia made this discovery years before she met her husband. She's often referred to by her married name of Cecilia Payne-Gaposchkin – it's worth knowing that if you decide to research her.

Janet Taylor – Leading Lady of Navigation

While her father was teaching maths and navigation
    Janet crept into the back of his class.
        Taunted by the boys behind her father's back
            she saved her clever questions for when
            they were alone.

He pointed out the constellations in the clear
Durham sky –
    Ursa Major – the Big Bear, Ursa Minor – the
    Little Bear,
        Pegasus – the Winged Horse, Orion – the
        Hunter.
    And Polaris – the Pole Star, guide to the north
showing her the way home.

Married and living in London she liked to be amongst
    the forest of masts down by St Katherine's Docks,
        her baby swelling in her belly,
her head sifting formulae.

She thought about the look-outs swaying in the
blinding storms,
>the crew pitching forward into seething sea.
>>Did they really think the carved figures lunging
>>>from the bowsprits could see through
>>>endless nights,
>could steer devils into wind and calm the roiling
>sea?
Surely she could help to keep them safe?

Her charts, tables, chronometers and sextants
>pointed to accurate routes,
>>mindful that the earth was flattened at the poles.
>>She saved more lives at sea than she
>>would ever know.

Chrissie Gittins

*Janet Taylor (1804–1870) was an astronomer, teacher of navigation,
mathematician, author, inventor and instrument maker. She owned a nautical
academy and a business which made and repaired navigational instruments.
She also had five children and three step-children.*

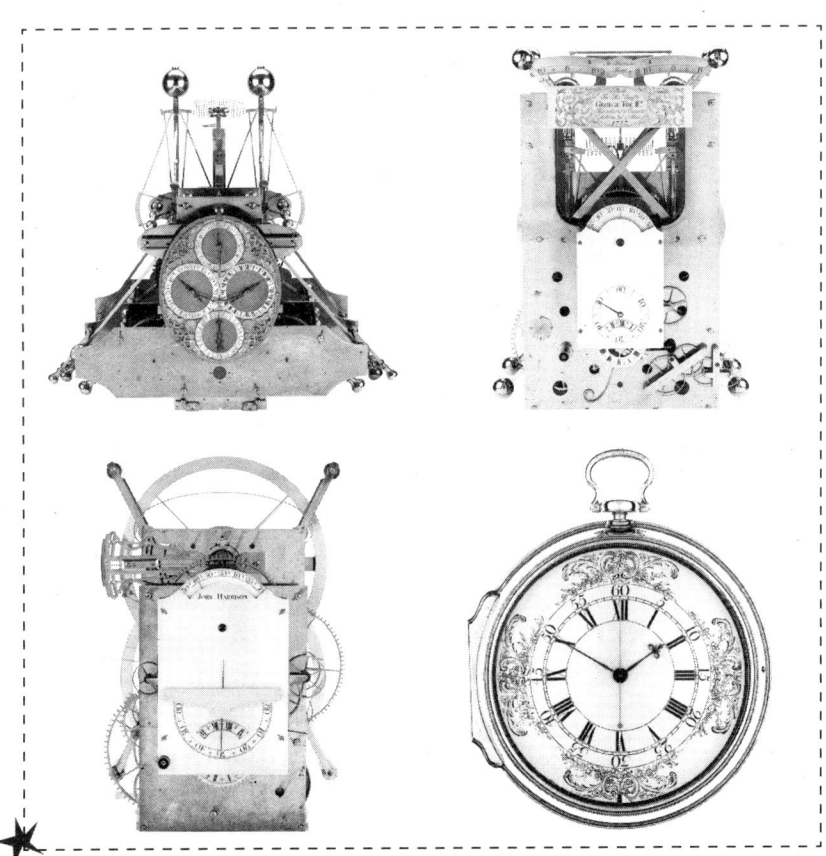

John Harrison's timepieces, clockwise from top left: H1, H2, H4, H3

Time

Emigravit

With sails full set, the ship her anchor weighs.
Strange names shine out beneath her figure head.
What glad farewells with eager eyes are said!
What cheer for him who goes, and him who stays!
Fair skies, rich lands, new homes, and untried days
Some go to seek: the rest but wait instead,
Watching the way wherein their comrades led,
Until the next stanch ship her flag doth raise.
Who knows what myriad colonies there are
Of fairest fields, and rich, undreamed-of gains
Thick planted in the distant shining plains
Which we call sky because they lie so far?
Oh, write of me, not 'Died in bitter pains,'
But 'Emigrated to another star!'

Helen Hunt Jackson

Photograph of Flamsteed House, the original home of the Astronomer Royal at the Royal Observatory, Greenwich, 2005

Time-Fall

The Time Ball rises

12:55: half-mast

On your marks
all tall ships in the harbour . . .

12:58: to the top

Stand ready-to-set
all clocks and chronometers
Londoners, officers, mariners, astronomers . . .

13:00: *Now!*

     the

     Time

     Ball

     falls

     down

     down

down

down

down

in

its

own

long

long

it

tud

in

al

line
calibrating
celebrating
navigating
time

Elena de Roo

Miss and The Time Ball

There's a bright red sphere
called a *time ball*
that rises and falls
at the Royal Observatory
on top of Flamsteed House
that just last week
we went on a school trip to see

I wandered around, just me
When I heard Miss say excitedly,
'*It was first used in 1833*
Fifty years before GMT'
I calculated quickly
'Back then Miss
I would have been
about minus . . .
180.'

And as the rest of the class
moaned about being bored
and hungry
sneaking each other sweets
saying they'd starve if they didn't eat
Miss sidled next to me
'*Watch!*' she smiled

At 12.55
as the time ball rose
halfway up the mast
we froze
we gasped
we laughed
Just Miss and I
'Imagine,' she sighed
'the ghosts of London sailors
who had long since sailed by
along the River Thames
using this miracle ball
to gauge and frame
the course of their days.'

Then at 12.58
as this sphere of time
climbed to the top of its mast
we craned our necks,
'The sailors back then
would only know their location
by celestial navigation
using old marine clocks
and every day at one
when the time ball dropped
they would look up at this site
from their ships sailing by
to make sure their chronometers
were absolutely right.'

The passion she had
for stars and time
sparked a part of my brain
that before I met Miss
had not been alive

And then, bang on one
the time ball fell
and Miss sighed, 'Oh Well
It's been lovely talking to you
You better get back
to your own class.'
She shook my hand
disappeared into the throng
and with that, Miss was gone

But what she'll never know
though I dream of telling her so
that from a minute after one
seconds after
she had disappeared into that throng
I had decided
Thanks to Miss & The Time Ball
As the clouds above Greenwich
made way for the sun
What, in the future
I would become

Mark Bird

FIG, 2.

Illustration of the Time Ball on top of
Flamsteed House, 1844

"GREENWICH MEAN TIME:" MRS. BELLEVILLE, WHO CHECKS THE HOUR DAILY AT THE GREENWICH OBSERVATORY FOR THE BENEFIT OF LONDON CLOCKMAKERS. (From a Photograph by Samuel A. Walker, 230, Regent Street.)

Photographic reproduction of Elizabeth Belville, also known as the Greenwich Time Lady

The Greenwich Time Lady

After Ruth Belville 1853–1943

It's just Arnold and I
walking the time
from Greenwich to Clerkenwell
walking the line
bringing the time
down the Docks, up the West End
over the river, round the bend

With Arnold by my side
I am always right
I keep him safe
he keeps me well paid
his face in my hand
his hands in my pocket
whatever the weather, we walk it

We walk through wars
we walk through threats –
radiowaves, the pips, Big Ben

All things end, our enemy is time
Arnold never dies

Anna Kisby

Arnold = Watch (she sold the right time)

The Question of Longitude

In a little town
on the banks of the Humber
John Harrison pays no heed
to how much time
he's spending making clocks.

On a ship
on several seas
John Harrison pays no heed
to how much time
he's spending on the Longitude problem.

In an observatory
on the banks of the Thames
John Harrison is celebrated
time after time.

Rob Walton

Print showing John Harrison, pioneering clockmaker who invented the marine timekeeper that helped solve the problem of finding longitude at sea, 1768

Tomorrow's another day

If you're always over-thinking
If your tired brain's full of chatter –
Just remember in 5,000,000,000 years,
That none of this will matter.

Sarah Ziman

Five billion years' time is when scientists think our sun will finally come to the end of its life, although life on Earth may 'only' have another billion years or so before things get seriously toasty.

Longitude

They drew a line around the world
A line no man could see
I prayed that you would find that line
And follow it home to me

I know not how Harrison's clock can work
Adrift on the featureless ocean
Or threads that enmesh the travellers all
From jungles to the lands frozen

I will never see the Earth's great circles
Only hear of the tropics and equator
All that matters are the lines you spoke of
And your return to our green acre

When the great storms spin the compass
And churn the waters black
I'll know that there is some safe way
To bring my sailor back

So, as you cross the hemispheres
And look to the stars above
Track those hidden lines my darling
And come home, my one true love

Dawn McLachlan

The Palace of Time

In the Palace of Time
giant gears engage
cogs the size of cartwheels.

They glisten with oil
shine brightly as burnished brass
whir and hum.

Seconds swarm like angry flies
on huge clock faces.

Minutes gently whisper greetings
hours drift into place
softer then falling leaves.

Days drop as evening rain
fills pools and puddles
twenty-four hours deep.

Weeks and months change into years
like caterpillars morphing into moths
or flickering butterflies.

The hands of the Eternal Clock rotate
counting out the moments.

Past, Present and the Future
look at each other, start to laugh
play hide-and-seek, running round
the attic's endless space.

In the Palace of Time
green light cracks the ball-room floor
Time's music plays an elegant dance.

All the windows circle the sun
and the beat goes wild, grows wilder.

Yellow, red and russet beams
shine on the dancers, then they freeze
and every window frosts.

Until sloping sundial shadows
measure another dawn.

David Harmer

The Tree and the Pool

'I don't want my leaves to drop,' said the tree.
'I don't want to freeze,' said the pool.
'I don't want to smile,' said the sombre man.
'Or ever to cry,' said the Fool.

'I don't want to open,' said the bud,
'I don't want to end,' said the night.
'I don't want to rise,' said the neap tide.
'Or ever to fall,' said the kite.

They wished and they murmured and whispered.
They said that to change was a crime.
Then a voice from nowhere answered.
'You must do what I say,' said Time.

Brian Patten

Holding Back Time

Last night we gained a jot of time,
Clocks were held to let
An extra second slip into our lives.

Time enough for feet to leave the ground,
For fingers to click,
For an unkind word to be said.

Time for a mouth to open,
For a bee to land on a zinnia,
For a door to slam after a row.

Time for an eye to blink,
For a finger to push a piano's Middle C,
For the penny to drop.

Time for an apple to drop from the tree,
For a swing to swing,
For someone to change their mind
About saying that unkind word.

We have a leap second to make use of,
A jumping off point into our world.
What will you do with it?

Chrissie Gittins

Every few years we gain a second – called a leap second – to keep up with the varying rotation of the Earth. The last leap second was introduced 31 December 2016.

Index of First Lines

Index of Poets

Acknowledgements

The compiler and publisher would like to thank the following for permission to use their copyrighted material:

Abbott, Matt: 'Diary entry, Greenwich – 10th August 1675' © Mark Abbott. Reproduced with kind permission of the author; **Benson, Gerard:** 'A Small Star' from *Wonder* chosen by Ana Sampson (Pan Macmillan, 2021) © Gerard Benson. Reproduced with kind permission from the estate of the author; **Bertulis, Debra:** 'Kepler'. Reproduced with kind permission of the author; **Bird, Mark:** 'Before I Close My Curtains' and 'Miss and the Time Ball' © Mark Bird. Reproduced with kind permission of the author; **Bromley, Carole:** 'Hailey's Comet' © Carole Bromley, 2025. Reproduced with kind permission of the author; **Brownlee, Liz:** 'The Moon' © Liz Brownlee, 2025. Reproduced with kind permission of the author; **Coats, Lucy:** 'The Myths of Space' and 'The Lady Computers' © Lucy Coats, 2025. Reproduced with kind permission of the author; **Coe, Mandy:** 'Animals Name the Constellations' first published in *Belonging Street* by Mandy Coe (Otter-Barry Books, 2020), 'Planets of Our Solar System, Named in Order from the Sun' previously unpublished and 'Bedtime Reading': previously unpublished © Mandy Coe, 2025; **Conlon, Dom:** 'Father Christmas Sent Me to the Moon', 'Native American Moons', 'What Am I?', 'This Rock, That Rock', 'For All Mankind' from *This Rock, That Rock* by Dom Conlon (Troika, 2020) and 'Moons' from *Astro Poetica* by Dom Conlon (Inkology, 2014) © Dom Conlon; **Cookson, Paul:** 'In My Sights' and 'The Loneliness of the Solo Astronaut' © Paul Cookson, 2025. With kind permission of the author; **Corbett, Pie:** 'Stars' and 'Light Years' © Pie Corbett. Reproduced with kind permission of the author; **Cowling, Sue:** 'Moon' © Sue

Cowling. Reproduced with kind permission of the author; **Davies, Nicola:** 'The Leviathan's Eye' and 'Komorebi' © Nicola Davies. Reproduced with kind permission of the author; **de Roo, Elena:** 'Expanding Forever' first published in *Shaping the World: 40 Historical Heroes in Verse* by Liz Brownlee: (Pan Macmillan, 2021); **Dean, Jan:** 'You Can't Just Point a Rocket at the Sky and Hope' and 'June 1963' first published in *Reaching the Stars* by Jan Dean, Liz Brownlee & Michaela Morgan (Pan Macmillan, 2017). Reproduced with kind permission of the author; **Denton, Graham;** 'Evening Shifts' and 'The First Man in Space' © Graham Denton, 2025. Reproduced with kind permission of the author; **Dougherty, John:** 'The Last Light of the Sun', 'Big Bang' and 'Cecilia' © John Dougherty, 2025. Reproduced with kind permission of the author; **Elson, Rebecca:** 'Aberration', 'What if There Were No Moon?', 'Let There Always Be Light', 'The Expanding Universe', and 'We Astronomers' from *A Responsibility to Awe* by Rebecca Elson (Carcanet, 2018) © Reproduced with permission from the publisher; **Harrold, A. F.:** 'The Point' from *The Book of Not Entirely Useful Advice* (Bloomsbury, 2020). Reproduced by kind permission of the author; **Gill, Nikita:** '93 Per Cent Stardust' from *Your Soul is a River* (Thought Catalog Books, 2016) © Nikita Gill. Reproduced with kind permission of the author; **Gittins, Chrissie:** 'Galileo' first published in *Spaced Out: Space Poems* chosen by Brian Moses and James Carter (Bloomsbury, 2019), 'Holding Back Time' first published in *Stars in Jars* by Chrissie Gittins (Bloomsbury, 2014) and 'What Caroline Herschel Remembers' and 'Janet Taylor – Leading Lady of Navigation' © Chrissie Gittins. Reproduced with kind permission of the author; **Hardy-Dawson, Sue:** 'Dazzle Dance' first published in *The Big Amazing Poetry Book* edited by Gaby Morgan (Macmillan Children's Books, 2022) © Sue Hardy-Dawson. Reproduced with kind permission of the author;

Harmer, David: 'The History of Nothing' from *Spaced Out* edited by Brian Moses and James Carter (Bloomsbury, 2019), 'Copernicus Kicked Up A Fuss', 'King Charles Discusses His Royal Observatory', and 'The Palace of Time' © David Harmer, 2025. Reproduced with kind permission of the author; **Howe, Sarah:** 'Relativity' commissioned by National Poetry Day; **Hulme, Jay:** 'You' from *Moonstruck*, Otter Barry Books; **Husband, Vicki:** 'Extremely Large Telescope' from *This Far Back Everything Shimmers* by Vicki Husband (Vagabond Voices, 2016) © Vicki Husband. Reproduced with kind permission of the author; **Jacob, Lucinda:** 'Dream Flight' from *Hopscotch in the Sky* (Little Island Books, 2017 © Lucinda Jacob. Reproduced with kind permission of the author; **Kisby, Anna;** 'Annie Maunder Explains the Sun'; some of these sun descriptions are Annie Maunder's own words, from her book *The Heavens and their Story* (1908) and some are inspired by Annie's solar photographs, and 'The Greenwich Time Lady: after Ruth Belville 1853-1943'. © Anna Kisby. Reproduced with kind permission of the author; **Lime, Attie:** 'We Have Spacedust In Our Hair' and 'Shades of Shooting Star' © Attie Lime, 2025. Reproduced with kind permission of the author; **Malaspina, Ann:** 'Vera's Questions' first published in *Tyger, Tyger Magazine*, 2023. Reproduced with kind permission of the author; **McLachlan, Dawn:** 'Moon Dance', 'Impossible Things' and 'Longitude' © Dawn McLachlan, 2025. Reproduced with kind permission of the author; **McLeod, Myles:** 'It Hurtled Down to Middlesbrough' and 'Chaika', poem by Myles McLeod, shape by Liz Brownlee from an idea by Myles McLeod from *Shaping the World*. Reproduced with kind permission of the author; **Morgan, Michaela:** 'Star!' © Michaela Morgan, 2025. Reproduced with kind permission of the author; **Moskowitz, Cheryl:** 'Brief Interview With a Gravitationally Completely Collapsed Object' and 'Census Taker of the Sky' © Cheryl Moskowitz. Reproduced with kind permission of the author; **Mucha, Laura:** 'The Lonely Side of the Moon' first published in *Dear Ugly Sisters and other poems*, Otter-Barry Books, and 'Looking Back'. Reproduced with kind permission of the author; **Newberry, Jane:** 'In the Chapel-Like Perfection of the Royal Observatory' and 'First Lady of the Stars' © Jane Newberry. Reproduced with kind permission of the author; **Nichols, Grace:** 'Moon-Mad' from *Cosmic Disco, Otter Barry Books*; **Morgan, J. O.;** 'We used to think the universe was made . . .' from *Interference Pattern* (Jonathan Cape, 2016). Reprinted by kind permission of the Penguin Random House Group; **Oliver, Rhiannon:** 'Always' and 'Your Host Today' © Rhiannon Oliver. Reproduced with kind permission of the author; **Patten, Brian:** 'The Tree and the Pool'. Reproduced with kind permission of the author; **Piercey, Rachel:** 'Aphelion' and 'Rosetta and the Singing Comet' © Rachel Piercey. Reproduced with kind permission of the author; **Ralleigh, Gita:** 'A Quark in the Dark' © Gita Ralleigh. Reproduced with kind permission of the author; **Rice, J. H.:** 'I am the silence' © J. H. Rice. Reproduced with kind permission of the author; **Rice, John:** 'What the Sun Said,' 'What the Moon Said,' 'What the Star Said' and 'The International Space Station Above Our House' © John Rice. Reproduced with kind permission of the author; **Sardelli, Darren:** 'Aurora Borealis' © Darren Sardelli, 2025. Reproduced with kind permission of the author, www.laughalotpoetry.com; **Shirtliff, Jacqueline:** 'The Pleiades' and 'Galileo' © Jacqueline Shirtliff. Reproduced with kind permission of the author; **Sirdeshpande, Rashmi:** 'A whole universe' and 'The Perseids' © Rashmi Sirdeshpande. Reproduced with kind permission of the author; **Stevens, Roger:** 'The Old Royal Observatory, Greenwich', 'Gazing Puzzle' and 'Halley's Comet'. Reproduced with kind permission of the author; **Varchol Perron, Lisa:** 'Telescope' first published in *Tyger, Tyger Magazine*, 2023. Reproduced with kind permission of the author;

Image credits